WAITING FOR THE HANGMAN

When Buck Armstrong agrees to take on the job of protecting a friend's friend, he has to accompany Vanessa Grange who is riding on the stagecoach to visit her Uncle Clarence. Unfortunately, however, he's in jail awaiting the hangman and must pay the price for his involvement with the Henry Plummer gang. Before that happens he wants Buck to help the girl find Plummer's hidden stash of stolen gold. But there are others around who also want the gold.

Books by Carlton Youngblood
in the Linford Western Library:

BUCK AND THE WIDOW RANCHER
THE RANGE SHOOTOUT
GOLD FOR DURANGO

CARLTON YOUNGBLOOD

WAITING FOR THE HANGMAN

Complete and Unabridged

LINFORD
Leicester

First published in Great Britain in 2009 by
Robert Hale Limited
London

First Linford Edition
published 2010
by arrangement with
Robert Hale Limited
London

British Library CIP Data

Youngblood, Carlton.
    Waiting for the hangman. - -
(Linford western library)
1. Western stories.
2. Large type books.
I. Title II. Series
823.9'2–dc22

ISBN 978–1–44480–439–3

Published by
F. A. Thorpe (Publishing)
Anstey, Leicestershire

Set by Words & Graphics Ltd.
Anstey, Leicestershire
Printed and bound in Great Britain by
T. J. International Ltd., Padstow, Cornwall

This book is printed on acid-free paper

1

At various times in his past, James Buckley Armstrong had herded cattle, horses and once even, sheep. He didn't like to talk about the sheep and in the future he didn't think he'd talk much about this job either. The girl sitting on the bench of the rocking stagecoach across from him was almost young enough to be his daughter, for gawd's sake.

Looking at her, his eyes hidden by the wide brim of his Stetson, he decided that might be stretching it a bit; just recently on the other side of thirty he certainly wasn't that old. Somehow, though, she did give the impression of being young and that didn't make him happy. He was a cattleman, for gawd's sake, not a nursemaid.

But what could he have done? James

Buckley Armstrong, called Buck by almost everyone who knew him, couldn't turn down Professor Fish when he was asked to take on the job of protecting the youngster. He owed the old man too much ever to say no. When the good professor needed help, his was the first hand that went up. As usual, it wasn't Prof Fish wanting help; it was one of the old codger's friends who needed looking after.

Buck didn't know what the old man was a professor of, or exactly what he did with himself, but he certainly had a lot of friends. This time it was the relative of the smooth-cheeked girl, long blonde braids hanging down the front of her light blue traveling dress he was watching out for. She was watching the world go by, her big blue eyes wide with excitement as the brown sand and gray sagebrush rolled by the coach's window.

'Gosh, Mr Buck,' even her voice was overflowing with excitement, 'there sure is a lot of . . . ' she hesitated a bit, then flashed a smile at him, 'a lot of nothing out here in the West, isn't there?'

Buck nodded and shoved the canvas curtain aside, stuck his head out the window and twisted around to check on his black stud horse tied to the back of the coach. The black didn't like being pulled along behind the coach but the big cowboy wasn't going far without him. They had been partners for a long time and understood each other. The horse was not a great beauty, hard-mouthed, strong-willed and pigheaded, showing a bad temper with everyone with the exception of Buck. And then only most of the time.

Unlike his horse, Buck Armstrong was nearly always happy, wearing a big smile either already plastered on his face or soon to be. Wearing his faded denim pants, the legs worn outside the tops of his dusty, scuffed pointed-toed riding-boots, and his long-sleeved calico shirt, the colors long since faded into muted hues, it was clear this was a cattleman. The .44 Colt Dragoon in its leather holster belted around his waist showed enough wear to warn any observant onlooker that this was a man who, although he smiled a lot, wasn't someone to mess with.

The portly man sitting across the coach from Buck and next to the young woman chuckled, causing his double chins to flutter. Buck had been keeping his eye on this fellow. From his clothes, the big cowboy figured the man was probably a banker or small-town business owner. Flat-heeled, black leather shoes gleaming with polish were firmly planted on the rollicking floor of the coach. His pinstripe woolen suit pants had the kind of crease that only came from the iron of a Chinese laundry and dry cleaners. A chain of thick, heavy-looking gold links hung in a curve from one pocket to another of the man's vest. The man was too proud of himself, Buck thought, and too quick to smile at Vanessa.

Vanessa. Who ever heard of a name like that? A city name, he guessed.

Good for a city girl, but, and here he frowned, wondering for the thousandth time how she was going to react to a town like French Gulch. He'd never been to this part of Utah, but he'd been in plenty towns just like it. He knew what to expect; a single, wide, dirt street with buildings on either side, mostly single-story with tall false-fronts opening out on to plank sidewalks. There'd probably be no more than a handful of businesses, just enough to supply the surrounding ranchers with the bare essentials. Not a place for a young, clean, sweet-smelling city girl, that's for sure.

'Is this your first time in the West?' the banker asked, keeping his smile bright and cheerful and his eyes on her face. Buck didn't say anything, but he didn't take his eyes off him, either.

'Oh, yes,' she said, turning and smiling politely. 'Isn't it wonderful? So big and . . . do you think we'll see any Indians?'

The banker chuckled again and

shook his head. 'Not likely, missy, not likely at all. There are still a few wild ones running around causing trouble, but not in this part of the country.' He glanced across at Buck and then turned back to the girl. 'But you needn't fear. This big man with his heavy Colt would be able to fight off any redskins who wandered by. Or any outlaws, for that matter.'

Buck didn't comment or let his gaze shift.

'Are the good citizens of French Gulch going to be blessed with your company?' the banker asked, once again smiling at the girl.

'I'll be in French Gulch for a short while before returning home to Denver. Mr Armstrong,' Vanessa nodded at the big man sitting across from her by way of introduction, 'is my bodyguard. My name is Vanessa Grange.'

'Employment any man would enjoy, I'm sure, Miss Grange.' The banker glanced at Buck quickly before even more quickly returning his gaze to the young woman. 'I don't wish to be nosy, miss, but I'm proud to say I have the honor to be the district judge for that part of our great territory and know just about everybody there. Judge Harold Cummings, at your service, m'am.' He bowed his head slightly before going on. 'My stop in French Gulch will be brief, but if I can be of service to you in your business to that fair community, please don't hesitate to ask.'

Not a banker or businessman, but a judge, Buck thought. That doesn't mean he can be trusted. There had been plenty times he'd come across men who made a practice of thumping a law book, or even once or twice a Bible, who were as shady as any mask-wearing highwayman.

'Oh, then you probably know my uncle.' She took her eyes off the judge to flash a smile at Buck as if to say, see I can get along without you and your gun. Turning back to the judge she explained, 'He has a small business in

French Gulch. My aunt Elizabeth was, well, I guess you'd say, a good friend. He wrote to her to say he was feeling poorly. We decided, well, I suppose I badgered Aunt Elizabeth a little, but I did so want to come West. I'm going to visit him until he's feeling better.'

That was one thing the girl and Buck had in common, their feeling that having him along was unnecessary. Vanessa had let both her aunt and Buck know she wasn't happy with having the tall, rough-looking man for a traveling companion. Aunt Elizabeth, a tall strong-chinned woman who stood with shoulders squared, sternly looking him over after reading the letter of introduction from Prof Fish, seemed to agree. Good, Buck thought. Maybe he could tell the professor to find someone else.

But it hadn't happened. The old woman accepted Buck as the one to protect her niece and neither Vanessa nor Buck could talk her out of it. Not that he tried very hard. After all, anything Prof Fish asked, he'd do.

'What's your uncle's name?'

'Clarence Handy, but he's not really my uncle. I just call him that. He and my Aunt Elizabeth were engaged to be married, but according to what I've been told, he just up and disappeared one day. Years later she received a letter from him asking if he could come back.' Vanessa stopped and giggled as she went on with her story. 'Aunt Elizabeth told him certainly not. You ran away and now you can stay away, she wrote him.' She stopped giggling and her face became serious. 'But when he wrote saying he was doing poorly, she thought maybe he should come to Denver. He wrote back saying he wasn't able to, so here I am, going to him.'

It was now Judge Cumming who was frowning. 'Handy, huh,' was all he said for a moment, then, looking as serious as a judge about to hand down a sentence, he continued. 'And not your actual relation, you say? Then, Miss Grange, I suppose I can tell you without dampening your spirit too much. It distresses me, miss, to inform you that Clarence Handy is in the French Gulch jail waiting for the arrival of the state hangman. He's been sentenced to hang, you see.'

2

Buck had handled a lot of different kinds of trouble for Prof Fish's friends, but never anything like this. Helping the owner of a small struggling stage line being driven broke by a gang of holdup men was one thing, even the time he was sent out to protect a paleontologist and his daughter turned out to be quite easy. But this was going too far. Playing nursemaid to a long-skirt-wearing young woman going across the Utah countryside to a small mining town was asking a lot.

Buck Armstrong had never been to French Gulch, but he'd heard about it. The town, like so many in the West, had started out when someone found gold in a nearby stream. The discovery brought all kinds of men, hoping in one way or another to cash in on the discovery. In a few years the gold

11

petered out and the town's population moved on, still seeking riches of one kind or another. For the next couple years French Gulch was no more than a couple weathered buildings and a dozen or so permanent residents. The warped-sided structures housed a near-empty general store, a saloon and dance hall, and a barbershop. A handful of men who had had the foresight to look beyond the quick riches of gold and had staked out large tracts of land for their cattle kept the town alive. Slowly, as the ranches prospered and other cattlemen came in and filed on the empty land, the town itself grew.

When the stage pulled up in a cloud of dust before the town's only two-story building, the hotel, Buck saw it was more than the wild untamed mining town he had expected. False-fronted buildings lined both sides of the wide dirt street, and most of the hitching rails just outside many of those had saddled horses or buckboards tied to them. It was Saturday. Go-to-town day for many of the ranch families who lived in the area.

'Let me give you a hand, miss,' Judge Cummings said, stepping down from the coach and offering a hand to Vanessa. Buck had been too busy looking over the town and had let the smiling round-faced man light down first.

'Thank you, sir.' The girl smiled and, holding her long skirt aside so she could see the little step, she balanced on the judge's pale, sausage-fingered hand and carefully clambered down.

'I expect you'll be staying at the hotel so I'll leave you. Quite possibly, once you've settled in a little, we can have dinner. I will call upon you. Until then, good day,' the judge said, tipping his hat and, picking up a large leather-strapped suitcase that had been handed down by the driver, he walked away down the street.

Standing and taking a minute to stretch his tall six-foot frame, Buck let his eyes take in the street. One of the newer buildings directly across the street had a welcoming sign hanging over the plank sidewalk: The Past Time saloon. Thinking about the cold beer he'd find in there made his mouth water.

'Are you going to help me with my trunk, Mr Armstrong, or simply stand and stare down the town?' Vanessa's quiet demand broke the vision Buck had been enjoying. Taking his time, the tall cowboy turned his head to look down at the girl.

Standing up with her fists placed squarely on her hips, she looked a little older than she had when sitting across from him in the coach. The blue traveling-dress outlined the curves of her young body, making Buck rethink his earlier estimate. It was a woman standing there looking directly at him with frown wrinkles creasing her forehead. He almost laughed at her bossy anger.

'Well, Miss Grange,' he said, mocking the careful words of the judge, 'I guess getting you and your trunk inside might be the right thing to do, don't you think?' He couldn't help but smile as his soft words took some of the annoyance and stiffness out of her body. Reaching down, he grabbed her trunk and, picking up his saddle-bags with his other hand, he started up the steps to the hotel's front door. Vanessa hurried to catch up.

The man behind the counter was thin in almost every aspect, from his long thin nose that ran down the center of his narrow face to the thinness of what hair he still had, combed carefully over his nearly bald head. The only outsized part of him that Buck could see was the pair of bulging eyes that passed slowly over the woman's body. They seemed to stick out even more when he looked up into the cold gray of Buck's gaze.

'Good afternoon, sir, ma'am.' He nodded, being careful not to look too hard at Vanessa again. 'Just come in on the stage, did you?'

'Nope,' Buck answered, placing the trunk on the floor. 'We flew in on the back of the tornado that just came through town.' He laughed at the look on the clerk's face. 'Of course we came in on the stage. And because the sign out there says this is a hotel, I'd guess we'd like to take a couple of your better rooms.'

'Oh, yes, rooms,' the clerk simpered, careful not to look at the young lady or into Buck's eyes again. 'Yes, this is a hotel and we have very clean rooms. The bridal suite is on the second floor and is our best. Two rooms with the facilities at the end of the hall.' The clerk swung the big black leather-bound register around for Buck to sign.

'Nope, not the bridal anything, young man,' Buck said, taking up the pen and signing the book: *Buck Armstrong and guest*. 'The best single room for the young lady and another down the hall for me.'

'Oh, yes.' The thin-faced clerk hesitated, then took two keys off a nail on the wall behind him and pointed up the stairs. 'Rooms 201 and 202 are up the stairs and to your right.'

He carried her trunk up to the room and set it on the stand next to the bed. 'I'll be taking care of my horse, Miss Vanessa. I'll look around and see what I can find out about your uncle. I'll knock on your door when I come back.' Leaving Vanessa in her room to freshen up, he dropped his saddle-bags on to the bed in the other room.

Standing out on the sidewalk again, Buck studied the sign above the old building next door. The Past Time Saloon looked like a comfortable place to spend the heat of the day. A good place to learn all about the trouble the girl's uncle was in, too. But, shaking his head, decided the first place to ask his questions was the jail.

Having found a stall for his black horse in the big barn at the end of the street, Buck hung his saddle over a rail and, making sure there was a bucket of water close by and the hay manger was full, patted the big black rump and walked back out into the afternoon sunshine.

He stopped by the tack room where the old man looking after the business sat unmoving behind a spindly-legged table, and paid for the stall.

'Guess I should tell you, my horse gets a little testy whenever anyone he doesn't know or like gets too close,' Buck warned the man. Leaning against the doorjamb, he carefully rolled a smoke and struck a wooden match against his pants leg. He lit the quirley before going on, looking the old man directly in the eyes to emphasize his words. 'I guess I'm about the only man he knows and most times that don't count for much. Long as we've been together, I've never been sure whether the black even likes me. I'd be very careful around him, is all.'

The old man didn't comment, just nodded his understanding of the warning before turning back to the tattered dime novel he was reading.

Sure that he'd done all he could, Buck turned away, dropped his cigarette butt into a water trough and walked back up the street.

Seeing the bars on the windows on either side of the door of one place told the big man where the jail was most likely to be. Instinctively he ducked his head as he stepped through the doorway. He had learned at an early age always to dip his head. Short carpenters built most doorways to be used by shorter men, his pa had told him. It was, the old man had explained, the short man's way to get back at those taller than themselves. Over the years Buck had found this to be true.

'Anything I can do for you?' The room was dark after being outside in the bright sunlight and Buck waited a bit for his eyes to adjust. From what light streamed through the dirty windows, he could see a young man sitting behind a dark-wood desk. When the seated man turned a little, Buck caught the gleam of a badge on his vest.

'Yep, I guess you can. I understand you have an old man locked up. One Clarence Handy. I'd like to talk with him.'

For a long time the lawman sat and stared up at Buck, not saying anything. Then, slowly pushing the chair back, he stood and placed both hands flat on the top of his desk.

'Now, why would you want to talk to old Clarence?' The lawman's voice was soft but firm.

'Well, Sheriff, I guess that's between him and me.'

'No, sir, he's in my custody and that makes it my business. And it's Marshal, not sheriff. Marshal William Tell Coleman.' The marshal's eyes didn't move but stared directly into Buck's.

Slowly Buck nodded, 'Well, maybe. Anyhow, I'm Buck Armstrong and I've got a young girl who is waiting over at the hotel. We came in on the stage from Denver to see this man, Clarence Handy. She's some kind of relative, it seems.'

'I didn't know old Clarence had any relations. He's never said anything about having any.' Coleman didn't move for a minute, then asked, a slight frown wrinkling his forehead, 'So what do you want to talk to my prisoner about?'

'Just wanted to learn why he's being held. It was some shock when old Judge Cummings said her uncle was due for a hanging.'

'You talked with Judge Cummings?'

'Rode in on the stage with him. He didn't explain too much, just enough to warn the girl.'

Coleman let a minute go by and then allowed his body to relax. Motioning to Buck to take a chair, he sat back down. 'I'll let you talk with him. You'll have to leave your Colt out here, though.'

Buck nodded. 'What's the old man been charged with, anyhow? I'm going to have to tell his niece something.'

'Ever hear of the Henry Plummer gang?' Buck nodded again. There weren't many people in the West not familiar with the Plummer gang. About a year earlier, Plummer and nearly two dozen men who were thought to be members of his gang had been hanged. The story made all the newspapers back East and had been the main topic of conversation throughout the West ever since.

According to the stories going around, Henry Plummer had been elected sheriff of a mining district farther up north. Soon after taking office there was a whole string of hold-ups and murders in the area. No arrests were ever made even after it became clear that Plummer probably had something to do with the crimes. Before any outside law could come in, a vigilante committee was formed, which rounded up those men who were suspected of being part of the gang. Within the first two months of that year, 1864, close to two dozen men were taken out and hanged. Most of those men were probably guilty but it was also believed that more than one innocent man was among them.

'Yeah, I guess everybody has heard about that event. What does Clarence Handy have to do with it?'

'Old man Handy came into town about the time all that robbing trouble began,' Marshal Coleman said, leaning back in his chair. 'He opened up a saddle shop and did all right. Didn't talk much, was mostly stand-offish. Kept to himself. A couple months ago, up in the Bannock mining district where the Plummer gang worked, a US deputy marshal arrested a man named George Ives. He was tried, convicted, and hanged for the murder of Nicholas Tiebolt. Going up the steps to the gallows, Ives laughed and claimed he had been one of Plummer's gang. The vigilantes hadn't caught them all, he said. There were still a few who had got away. One of them, he claimed, was an old man named Clarence Handy.'

Buck grimaced at the news. How the hell was he going to tell Vanessa that Uncle Handy had been a member of the notorious Plummer Gang?

3

The jail cell Handy was in was at the very back of the building. Through a door, the top half of which was a windowless barred opening, four six-foot square cells ran along one side leaving enough room for a narrow hallway. Each cell was simply a box of which the walls were no more than iron bars. Handy lay on his back on a flat bench in the last cell.

Buck had left his Colt on the marshal's desk. He had the sensation of being a little off balance without the five pounds of machined steel hanging from his hip. Aware of being weaponless, he felt almost naked. Standing in front of the cell door looking down at the sleeping man, he couldn't help but keep his big right hand on the empty holster.

'Wal, ya just come back to stare or ya

got somethin' to say?' The man lying on the bench said, without looking up. The words sounded raspy and were followed by a bout of coughing. Handy sat up and leaned over until the hacking cough stopped.

Buck waited until the old man breathed easier again. Neither spoke for a time, both men looking the other over.

'What do ya want,' Handy asked softly, almost whispering.

Wearing a pair of worn bib overalls, the old man's face was lined and sun-darkened. The back of the hand that held a dirty-looking faded red handkerchief was liver-spotted.

'Seems you wrote a letter to the woman who had almost become your wife,' Buck said, cussing himself for not asking the girl what her Aunt Elizabeth's full name was.

Handy looked long and hard at Buck before responding. 'Yeah. Dunno why I wrote her. Knew when I did it there'd only be trouble. Guess I just wanted someone to know where I had been. Didn't think she'd send anyone out to see what a mess of things I'd made. So, ya can go on back and tell her ya saw me just before they hung me up to dry.'

'Nope, I'm not the one who came out to see you. I'm just looking after a young woman who has that job. Name's Vanessa Grange. She's the niece of the woman in Denver.'

'I figured Lizzy woulda forgotten me by now,' Handy muttered. 'I don't know no niece of her'n. Not that it matters, now. Tell the young woman to go on back and give my last regards to Lizzy.' He pulled the hanky from a back pocked and covered his mouth as a fit of coughing stopped his words.

'That cough sounds bad, old-timer. Have you been in here long enough to catch a cold?'

'Nope, it's been bothering me a spell. That don't matter neither. Go along now. I don't feel like talking anymore.' Not bothering to look at Buck, Handy lay back on the hard bench and put his hat over his face. For a long moment the big man stood looking down at the prisoner, hearing his rasping breathing. Then he turned and walked back toward the marshal's office.

'Man's got a bad cold, Marshal,' he said. He picked up his revolver and, after checking the loads, slipped it back where it belonged. Not getting a response, but feeling more comfortable, he squared his hat and nodding his thanks to the lawman, went back out on to the street.

Well, he said to himself, I certainly didn't learn much there that'll help me explain things to the girl. Maybe it's time for a drink.

The Past Time saloon was typical of small-town taverns. A long bar ran along one wall with liquor bottles lined up on shelves behind it. A scattering of small round tables, each with two or three chairs, filled the other half of the room. Against the back wall a few larger tables had been placed, each with its own lantern hanging over it and each covered with felt. On those tables, decks of cards lay waiting for the next poker game.

Having found a place along the bar, not too far from the nearest customer but still far enough not to appear unfriendly, Buck ordered a mug of beer from the round-bellied bartender. His first swallow was long and satisfying, the cool malty-tasting brew cutting through the dryness of his throat. After wiping the foam from his upper lip, he placed the half-emptied glass on the bar and leaned with one elbow resting on the wood. He turned a little and surveyed the room.

Men sat at a few of the tables, glasses of whiskey in front of some, others nursing schooners of beer. At one of the poker tables in back, Buck saw a man sitting alone laying out his cards in a game of solitaire.

'That'd be Amos, playing cards by hisself, waiting for someone to come along.' The information came from the man standing a short way down the bar from Buck. 'I seen you get off the afternoon stage and made a bet with myself as to how long it'd take until you came through the door.'

Buck smiled. 'And did you win your bet?'

''Course I did. I always win when I bet with myself.' The other man laughed and slid his beer glass down next to where Buck stood. It was obvious from the man's clothes that Buck was talking to one of the town's business owners. From the toes of flat-soled shoes peeking out from the bottom of his dark-wool pants, to the white long-sleeved cotton shirt, this was a town man, not a rancher.

'Harold Sims is my name,' the man introduced himself, sticking out a hand. 'I'm the town barber. My shop is across next to the hotel, if you find yourself in need of a haircut or professional shave.'

'I'll remember that,' Buck said, taking the offered hand. 'Buck Armstrong's my name. And you're right, after eating the dust churned up inside that stagecoach, a cold beer was about the first thing I had on my mind.'

For a while neither man spoke, sipped his beer and rested against the bar. Emptying his glass, Buck motioned to the barkeep for another and to pour one for his newfound friend.

'Thanks. Guess when you come in for a haircut I'll have to give you a good deal.' The barber laughed and lifted his glass to toast the big man.

'I heard there's a bad man in the jail over there, waiting for the hangman. What's that all about?' Buck asked after a few minutes.

'Well, yes. Old Handy was convicted of being a member of the Henry Plummer gang. Most folks up north thought they'd seen the end of those boys, but must've missed a couple. One of them laughed just before taking the big drop and boasted of knowing at least one more the vigilantes had missed. Named our own Clarence Handy. A good man with his knives when it comes to working leather, but, well, guess the good people of French Gulch didn't like having a road agent so close by. Even an old-timer like Clarence.'

'So now they're going to hang him. Guess it doesn't pay to have someone spout out your name just when that someone is going to get hung.'

'Ah, well. It didn't help that Clarence all but admitted to being one of the gang. He just wouldn't say yes or no when the judge asked him. So the jury called him guilty and the marshal sent for the hangman. The town council went ahead and built a gallows down on the other side of the stable; now all they need is the expert with the ropes.'

'I must've not seen the gallows when I put my horse away. When is the hangman expected to get here?'

'Dunno. The marshal sent out a telegram, but I don't know much more than that. Some folks around town think the town needs a good saddle-maker more than a hanging, but I think anyone guilty of robbing and killing gets what they deserve.'

Buck couldn't think of anything else to say so he just sipped more of his beer. He was about to toss back the last of it when he spotted a woman coming down the stairs in the back of the room. A tall woman in a long, black riding-skirt, the kind that allowed the wearer to set astride. Her blouse was long-sleeved, white with a ruffled front. Her hair, braided in an intricate pattern, hung far down her back, was the color his mama would call strawberry blonde.

As she came down she let her eyes sweep around the barroom, as if counting the number of customers. When her glance reached Buck, her eyes stopped. The big man slowly pushed away from the mahogany and, standing tall, stood frozen, feeling like a deer caught in a hunter's sights.

'Yeah, don't think you're the only one aware of her,' Sims said, his voice soft and his eyes not leaving her as she left the stairs and turned to the man playing solitaire. 'Ain't a man in town that don't dream of Molly Mae.'

'Molly Mae,' Buck said her name, letting it roll around his tongue like a piece of hard candy. 'She work here?' he asked.

'Not likely. Owns the place. Been running the Past Time since her husband was killed.' Seeing he had an audience, the barber went on with his story. 'Freddy Ralston was his name. Known by many around here, but never to his face, as Slick Freddy. One night he dealt one too many cards from the bottom of the deck and someone caught him. We all thought that'd be the end of the Past Time. Figured the widow would look around for a buyer. We all figured wrong. She closed the doors for a couple days and when she opened them, she had hired a helper. That's him sitting at that table. Name's Amos.'

Buck looked the man over but couldn't make out much about him.

'Seeing as you're new around here,

here's a bit of warning. That Amos is a big moose of a man with hands the size of dinner-plates. First off we all thought he might be something more than her hired man, but she made it clear: Amos was Molly Mae's bodyguard. And it only took one jasper to get out of line for us to learn that the big man's hands might look big and clumsy but they aren't. His fingers are long and flexible. Amos was dealing poker at that table as he does every night, when the fool across from him put his hand on Molly Mae's hip as she walked by. The idiot learned real quick that whether dealing cards or pulling the walnut-handled Colt .44 from his shoulder holster, Amos's hands could move like a striking rattler. The fool almost wet his pants when he looked up to find hisself looking into the black hole of Amos's revolver just inches from his nose.' Sims stopped his story to let Buck visualize the action.

'Oh, it happened,' Sims said after a bit. 'I was sitting at the table that night and I saw it. The fool's hand jumped from Molly Mae's hip like it was the top of a hot wood-stove. And his face was all white and sweaty, as if he was sitting right on top of that stove, too. It was something to see, I'll tell you. He very carefully put both hands flat on the table and stood up. Not taking his eyes off the unwavering barrel pointing at him, and not even picking up his chips, he started backing away, turning after a few feet and running through the swinging saloon doors into the night. He's never been back since. It was something to see, all right. But the best part was Amos. I was watching him. His face didn't show a thing. His revolver just seemed to slide back into the leather and he picked up the cards and started shuffling them. Just as if nothing had happened.'

Buck hadn't taken his eyes off the blonde woman while Sims talked. He had never let a woman get close to him, but somehow he knew that this one could cause him trouble.

4

Shaken by his reaction to the saloon owner's appearance, Buck thought it was time to go about his business. He left a few coins on the bar, nodded to the barber and turned without another glance toward the back of the barroom and pushed through the saloon doors.

The sun had moved closer to the far horizon while he'd been inside and he realized it was getting close to supper-time. Noticing a sign down the street that bore the single word, *Restaurant*, he decided that over a meal would be the best time to tell Vanessa what he'd learned about her uncle.

The supper menu was simple, beef-steak, ham or stew. Buck was quite happy when his steak, almost covering the entire white porcelain plate, was cooked as he liked it — burnt on the outside, blood-red in the middle.

Vanessa wasn't so easily satisfied. Stew as she knew it was not anything near what she was served, a huge bowl filled with bite-sized chunks of meat, carrots and potatoes all in a thick gravy. Not, she thought, the kind of meal a lady was expected to enjoy. By the time Buck had used a biscuit to sop up the last of the gravy that had covered the boiled potatoes which, along with a pile of steamed vegetables, had come with his steak, Vanessa had only managed a few small bites of her meal.

Right away, when the waitress, a large woman who was openly flirting with a couple cowboys sitting at a nearby table, had delivered their food, Buck had been aware of Vanessa's unhappiness.

'Something wrong with your stew?' he asked, ready to call the waitress back.

'No. I guess I'm just not hungry,' she responded, wondering exactly what she had gotten herself into, coming to French Gulch.

Until now she had never been farther west than the outskirts of Denver. Actually she had never been east of that big city either. When the opportunity came to travel, to experience something other than her hometown, she took it. What was a girl to do? Most of her friends, after graduating from Miss Engle's Seminary for Young Ladies, had either gotten married, gone on East to one of the big colleges or left on a European tour. Vanessa couldn't afford either college or a trip overseas and she didn't want to marry any of the eligible men in her social circle. Clarence Handy's letter came just in time.

Only to find out that the man Aunty Elizabeth had almost married was about to be hanged. This wasn't how she had thought it would be. The globules of grease she saw floating on top of the stew was almost all she could handle.

That was before Buck told her what he'd learned at the jail.

Sitting back in his chair and savoring

a large mug of black coffee, he thought about the best way to explain the way things were with her uncle. Well, he decided, if the water is cold, the best way is to just grit your teeth and jump in.

'I stopped to talk with the town marshal about your uncle. The news, I'm afraid, isn't good.' Buck stopped to sip the coffee, watching Vanessa's face for her reaction.

The tea she had asked for was too hot to drink but it gave her someplace to keep her eyes. People came and went amid loud laughter and she felt all alone, hearing about how the man she'd came to meet was going to be hanged.

'What did he do that was so bad?' she asked at last, dreading the worst.

Briefly Buck explained about how the Henry Plummer gang had been robbing and killing and how a bunch of vigilantes had done what they thought the law wasn't able to do. It was a hard story to tell the young woman and he didn't know any way to sugar-coat it.

'I'm sorry, but according to the marshal, when the judge asked if your uncle had anything to say in his defense, he didn't deny being part of the gang.'

Vanessa sat and thought about what she should do. Depressed and tired from the day's journey in the stage-coach, she worked out that all she could do was visit with Uncle Clarence. At least she could take that back to Denver and Aunt Elizabeth.

'It's pretty late for a visit tonight,' Buck said, seeing how exhausted she was. 'Probably be best if you got a good night's rest and after breakfast in the morning I'll introduce you to Marshal Coleman.'

After paying for their meals and walking her back to the hotel, Buck sat for a while in one of the rocking-chairs on the hotel porch. Rolling a quirly, he sat smoking and watched as the town settled in for the night. Like most Western towns, French Gulch, as the saying goes, rolled up the sidewalks soon after the sun went down. A few of the businesses, such as the hotel behind him or the saloon across the street, boasted lighted windows, but most of the rest of the buildings were dark.

Flicking the stub of his cigarette out into the street, he thought about going over to the Past Time for a last drink before going to bed. Remembering the blonde-haired tavern owner, he changed his mind. Checking on his horse would be a mite safer. Somehow just seeing that woman had caused his stomach to roll over and sweat to break out on his forehead. He didn't know if that was a good feeling or not and didn't want to find out. Not tonight, anyhow.

Walking down to the stable, he nodded to the old man who was still sitting at his small table, reading his book, a tattered Beadle's Dime Novel by the light of a kerosene lantern.

'That black horse of yourn is almost more trouble than I want in here, cowboy,' the old man complained.

Standing in the doorway, looking at the seated man, Buck saw that the frayed book was entitled *Maleaska, the Indian Wife of the White Hunter*, though the title was barely readable on the well-thumbed cover.

'Well, he's not that bad, if you don't try to get too close to him. You got a corral out back?' When the stableman nodded, Buck smiled. 'Then I'll just let him get familiar with it. You won't be bothered then.'

★　★　★

Sharing breakfast the next morning with the young woman wasn't much better than supper had been the night before. Vanessa Grange did eat better, though, going through her eggs and ham like she hadn't eaten in weeks. She even went so far as to ask for a second cup of tea when Buck, using a biscuit to wipe up a smear of egg yolk, settled back with a refill of his coffee. Buck was taking his time because he didn't look forward to walking the girl over to the jail.

Afraid his stomach would gurgle if he drank another cup of coffee, he put down his empty cup at last and frowned at the girl, now waiting patiently on the other side of the table.

'Guess you're wanting to go visit your Uncle Clarence,' he said, not asking but hoping she would have changed her mind overnight.

'Yes.' Her voice was stronger after the meal than it had been the night before. 'Mr Armstrong, I want you to know I don't look forward to this any more than you do. I'm sorry, but I do have to talk with him. Aunt Elizabeth will want to know, so I feel I have to do this. It's more than you asked for, and, well, I'm sorry.'

Buck looked at her and slowly nodded. Maybe, he thought, she wasn't such an empty-headed little girl after all.

'Yeah, well, let's get it done.'

After introducing her to Marshal

43

Coleman, Buck shucked his Colt and waited for the lawman to unlock the barred door. Carrying one of the office's wooden chairs for the girl to sit on, Buck followed Vanessa and the marshal down the narrow hall to the last cell.

'Hey, Clarence,' Coleman called out, 'you've got a couple visitors.'

'Don't know if I want any.' Buck heard the raspy voice and wondered about how bad the man's cold was. Not that it would matter long, he said silently.

'Mr Handy? I'm Vanessa Grange. I was raised by my mother's sister, Elizabeth Oskar.'

For a long minute the two stood looking at each other through the bars. When the marshal turned back toward his desk, Buck nodded.

'Miss Grange, I'll be with the marshal. Call if you need anything.' Nodding to the old man who stood in his stocking feet holding his dingy handkerchief in one hand, he placed the chair to one side and followed the lawman.

Coleman sat down behind his desk and watched as Buck took another chair.

'Tell me about the girl,' the marshal said.

'Well, I can't tell you much,' Buck said, turning his hat in one hand using the other to work on shaping the brim. 'I was asked by a friend to watch after her on this trip. That's about all I know. She lives with her aunt in Denver and, well, that's about it.' Smiling at the thought, he went on after a bit, 'Oh, and she doesn't like the stew put out over in the restaurant.'

'There's coffee on the stove and cups under the shelf,' Coleman offered, pointing to the enameled pot sitting on the pot-bellied stove. 'Help yourself.'

Nothing more was said until Buck had poured himself a cup and refilled the marshal's. The big man sat down again and blew on the hot coffee before taking up the conversation.

'A fellow over in the Past Time mentioned your having sent off for the hangman. Any idea when that fella will get here?'

'No,' Coleman answered, 'that's something else we can thank the Henry Plummer gang for, or at least the vigilantes. When the newspapers back East got a hold of the story all hell broke loose up in the capitol. The territorial governor up in Salt Lake City is fighting to get Congress to form Utah as a state. Those folks back East don't like the idea because of old Brigham Young and his Mormons. Then, on top of that, there come the stories of hooded vigilantes hanging nearly two dozen men without benefit of a judge or a preacher. Next thing you know, Young's appointed an official hangman to go around the territory and do the dirty work in an official way. So now we got to wait until he gets down here to us.'

Buck sipped his coffee. 'Guess he's got a lot of business, from what I hear about them Mormons. Hard enough, I guess, to keep one wife happy, but Brigham Young's menfolk like to have a number of wives. Sounds to me a sure-fire road to a hanging.'

Vanessa pushed through the barred door before either man could make any further comment.

'Marshal, Uncle Clarence is in need of a doctor,' she demanded. 'That's not just a cold he's got, he's spitting up blood.'

5

When it all got settled Buck had to agree; Vanessa Grange had a streak of stubbornness that knocked down everything in its way. Persuading the marshal to call for the town doctor was the first obstacle; Marshal Coleman was sure the old man just had a bad cold.

'Are you a medical expert, Marshal?' she asked. Watching from where he stood, Buck could almost swear he saw sparks flying from her eyes. 'You two are sitting out here in the sunshine while that old man is back there coughing his lungs up. I tell you, he's in bad shape.'

Marshal William Tell Coleman might be the strong representative of the law but before the storm named Vanessa he didn't have a chance. The next hurdle was almost too much for even her, though. Old Doc Saunders was the best available man for more than two days' ride in any direction; when it came to a medical decision his word was final.

After winning her argument with the marshal, Vanessa had demanded that he go get the doctor. Turning back to the cellblock, she left Buck alone in the marshal's office. He had just poured himself another cup of the strong coffee when Doctor Saunders, followed by the marshal, came barreling through the door. Not slowing down or paying any attention to Buck, the medical man pushed through the barred door and disappeared down the corridor. Marshal Coleman sighed and leaned a hip on the corner of his desk. For a few minutes the office was quiet, then the doctor called for the keys to the cell.

Marshal Coleman grabbed the ring of cell-door keys and, throwing a frown in Buck's direction, went to open the cell. Buck just naturally followed and watched as the doctor, with his stethoscope moving from place to place on the old man's chest, listened.

Vanessa was seated on the end of the bench with her uncle's head in her lap. Handy's eyes were closed.

There was no change in the dour expression on the doctor's face when he finished his examination. Replacing his medical tools in the black bag he carried, he stood up and, not saying anything to the prisoner, walked out of the cell. Vanessa gently put the man's head down on the bench and followed the marshal out of the cell. Marshal Coleman locked the cell door and followed Buck back into the office where he found everybody waiting.

'Well, Doctor, what is the verdict?' Marshal Coleman asked, standing next to his desk.

'Consumption,' Doc Saunders said abruptly. 'The signs are all there. He's got a fever, his face has an unhealthy pale look and his cough is harsh and unrelenting.' To make sure they all knew what he was saying, the doctor went on to explain. 'Consumption is a disease that eats up the lungs. I can't tell you where it comes from but that's the name it's been given, probably because, unless the patient gets treatment, the disease just seems to consume them from within.'

'What treatment can Uncle Clarence be given?' Vanessa's face was almost as pale as her relative's had been.

'Fresh air, sunshine. He shouldn't be kept in that dank corner of the building, for one thing. If he were my patient, I'd keep him in bed, lots of rest.'

Marshal Coleman shook his head. 'He's still my prisoner, Doc. Sentenced to hang. He'll have to stay in that cell until the hangman gets here.'

Vanessa wasn't having any of that. 'Why? If he has been sentenced, then he's been sentenced. But that's no reason for him to be tortured. He's just a sick old man,' she pleaded, 'and until your hangman arrives then he should be treated like any other sick person.'

Not giving anyone a chance to interrupt, and losing the pleading sound in her voice, she turned back to the doctor. 'Where would you treat him, if he walked into your office, Doctor?'

For a minute Doc Saunders stared at the young woman, then, with a small smile of defeat, he nodded.

'In my clinic,' he answered. 'Whenever I get a patient who can't be moved, I put him to bed in my front bedroom. I've got a woman who comes in to clean and cook for me; she helps me when needed as my nurse.'

'Now wait a minute,' the marshal cut in. 'That man back there is my prisoner. That means he stays in his cell until . . . well, until I'm told to take him out. That's all there is to that.'

'And who would be the one to tell you to take him out?' Vanessa asked.

'The judge, of course.'

'Then let's go see the judge, shall we?' Buck thought she had never sounded so sweet and determined. Remembering their meeting with Judge Harold Cummings on the stagecoach, he smiled inwardly. Already she had gotten her way with the marshal and the town doctor. It'll be interesting, he thought, to see how the good judge makes out. He decided not to go along with Vanessa and the doctor to see Judge Cummings. Better, Buck thought, if he let things happen without his help. That way, if, as he expected, the decision was to leave Handy safely locked up, he wouldn't have to face Vanessa's anger. Without talking about it, Marshal Coleman had the same thought and invited the big man to share a beer or two at the Past Time saloon. It was getting on to lunchtime, but the idea of a cold beer sounded better.

The two men stood against the long mahogany bar, nursing their mugs of the foamy brew and talked about everything except Vanessa and her uncle.

'I don't want you to make the wrong judgment about our good doctor,' Coleman said after all the talk about the weather, cattle prices and local law problems had been discussed. 'Doc Saunders is a good man and a good doctor,' Coleman added after a long silence. 'He never was as hard and crusty before his wife died. When Maude Saunders took sick and he couldn't do anything about it, he just changed. That happened just about a year ago. She died. It hit him hard. She was given a big send-off; nearly everybody in town was at the funeral. For a while we thought to let him grieve. Anyone got sick, they just suffered through it. Give him time, people said, and they did. But old Doc had about given up his treating of the area's residents. For a long time he just sat in an old rocking-chair on the front porch, grief-stricken.'

Coleman sipped his beer before going on with his story. 'It was little Mary Durey's falling sick that brought him out of it. Her pa brought his young daughter to the doctor and, not taking no for an answer, simply walked past him and on into the house. He placed his little girl gently on the doctor's leather couch and stood looking down at her.

'Someone happened to see it and said later that Doc Sanders had watched the man stride up the porch stairs and into his house. Slowly he got out of the rocker and, all bent over like an old man, he stepped into the doorway and stopped. Well, he knew Carl Durey, everybody did. He runs the general store. Married to the banker's daughter. Eloise Conrad, as she was before the marriage. The Dureys had just the one child, little Mary.

'The way the story went, Doc Saunders stood there, not making a sound. Then he shook himself as if waking from a bad nightmare, took his black medical bag from a table and went to the girl. Taking her wrist he pulled a turnip watch from his vest pocket and counted. I guess,' Coleman said, 'it took something like that for him to climb out of his miseries.'

Buck emptied his glass and motioned

for the bartender to bring a couple more. 'What happened to the little girl?'

'Oh, she came out of it OK. Had a fever for a while but she got better. The doctor thought she'd probably been bit by a spider or something.' He took a sip of beer before going on. 'Before his wife died, Doc Saunders wasn't like he is today. He had a big smile for everyone and was cheerful. Not the old grouch you saw.'

The two men were silent for a bit, each thinking his own thoughts. Buck's were on Molly Mae. Coming into the saloon with the marshal, Buck had quickly scanned the big room, looking for the blonde-haired owner. As before, Big Amos was sitting alone at a table in the back, but there was no sign of Molly Mae. Leaning against the bar, Buck made conversation with the lawman and tried to keep his eyes away from the stairs or the rooms up at the end of them.

Not meaning to talk about her, Buck was surprised when Marshal Coleman brought up her name.

'Have you met Molly Mae yet?'

'Uh huh. She introduced herself to me yesterday. A very attractive woman,' was all he could say.

'Yeah. A little too old for me; not that Big Amos would let me get near her.' Coleman laughed. 'But she's sure a looker, all right.'

'Big Amos. That's the big galoot sitting back there playing cards by hisself?'

The marshal turned his head to look, then nodded. 'Yep, that's him. Always sitting there, playing solitaire or dealing poker. And always between Molly Mae and any man brave enough to get ideas about her.'

Taking his eyes off the empty stairs, Buck took to studying the bottom of his beer mug.

'He's a big one, all right,' he murmured. Standing six feet tall himself, it wasn't often he came across men taller. At about 200 pounds, and little of that not muscle, Buck was a big

57

man himself. But having only seen Big Amos that once, he knew the woman's guardian was bigger. And possibly stronger. He didn't want to find out.

The two had just finished their drinks and were trying to catch the bartender's attention when the saloon doors swung open, letting the bright daylight stream in. It took a second or two for them to realize it was Vanessa standing there, holding the doors open.

'Here,' Marshal Coleman rushed to her side, putting an arm around her shoulders and turning her back out on to the porch. 'It isn't fitting for a lady like you to be going in there,' he explained, dropping his arm.

'Well, I don't know why not,' she said, defiantly. 'That's where you and Buck are and you're the one I want to talk to. Anyway, I saw another woman coming down the stairs.'

Buck had turned when the door opened but as the marshal moved to take Vanessa outside he had seen Molly Mae coming down the stairs. He watched as she stopped to speak to Big Amos, wondering whether she would come over to the bar. Without thinking about his beer mug being empty, he started to lift it to his lips, never taking his eyes off the blonde saloon owner, when Marshal Coleman opened the doors and called to him.

'Hey, Buck. You had better come listen to this,' he said. Then, before Buck could wave him away, he turned back through the doors.

'Damn,' Buck muttered. He put down the beer mug, dropped a few coins on the bar and headed outside.

'Well, somehow she did it,' Marshal Coleman said as Buck joined the pair. 'Judge Cummings says I can move Handy over to the doc's house.'

'I simply pointed out that Uncle Clarence is too sick to try to escape,' Vanessa explained. 'Anyway, it doesn't seem right that he should be hanged if he's so sick, does it? Judge Cummings agreed with me on that and said even if the hangman comes into town today, he wouldn't be allowed to do his work until the prisoner is well and able.'

Both Buck and the marshal shook their heads. 'Well, I can't go against what the judge orders,' Coleman stated. 'Buck, little Vanessa here asks that we get a buckboard to move her uncle. Do you mind going down to the livery stable and hitching one up?'

'Little Vanessa?' This time Buck was sure he saw sparks. 'I'll have you know, I'm not little anything, Mister Marshal.' Before she could grow even angrier, Buck mumbled something about getting a buckboard and walked away from the two.

6

Moving the old man down the street to the doctor's house, and then getting him settled in the front bedroom, took the efforts of all three. Handy, wearing a pair of iron handcuffs, was wrapped in blankets and laid out on the bed of straw in the back of the flat wagon Buck had gotten from the livery. Vanessa made sure she rode back there with the old prisoner, holding his head on her lap.

Clarence Handy didn't know exactly what to think about it all. Here he'd gotten himself all ready to take the big drop when this pretty little filly took over. Stretching out on the feather mattress with the marshal, Doc Saunders, the girl and some big stranger watching every move, he shook his head.

'I don't reckon I understand what

this is all about, but it's sure softer than that bench in the jail, I'll tell you,' he said. Then he fell into a fit of coughing and covered his mouth with a big linen handkerchief handed him by the girl.

Thanking her with his eyes, he tried to smile. 'I'm afraid I'm going to make a die of it. I'm going to create a vacancy, but it's a lot better to do it here than back in that cell.'

Doc Saunders, holding his arms out, herded everyone from the room. 'OK, now he's here and he's my patient. Marshal, you won't have to worry about him going anywhere, it'll be a long time before he can get up out of that bed.'

'He will get better, won't he?' Vanessa asked, worry wrinkling her forehead.

'Rest and a good diet of healthy food will help him,' Saunders assured her. 'The disease is pretty far gone, though, so don't expect any miracles. There's a good chance he'll pull through, but it's equally likely he won't. Only time will tell. Now, you all go on about your business and let me take care of mine.'

'Well, just so you know,' Marshal Coleman said, as he left the doctor's house, following behind Buck and Vanessa, 'I'm not sure this is a good idea. He's still sentenced to hang, and we can't overlook that. I'm going to drop in every so often to make sure my prisoner is still my prisoner.'

Without saying anything, Buck climbed into the buckboard and turned it back toward the livery stable, leaving the others to walk. Even though he'd only had the wagon for a few minutes, the old man at the stable still demanded his half-dollar.

'You rented it, didn't you?' he insisted. 'I coulda maybe rented it to someone else in that time you had it. Of course I'm gonna charge you rent on it.'

Shaking his head, Buck was digging in a pants pocket for the money when a horseman rode up and climbed out of the saddle.

'Gentlemen,' he said, stretching his back and stomping his feet to get the circulation flowing. 'I don't want to interrupt, but could I leave my horse here for a few days?'

'You sure can,' the old stable keeper said, grabbing the horse's reins. 'I'll take him back to a stall and rub him down. Feed him a bait of oats, too. It'll cost you four bits and another four bits for the stall overnight.'

'Sounds good to me, and I'm sure my horse will appreciate it, too.' Pulling a pair of heavy looking saddlebags off the animal, he smiled. 'Could one of you point me in the direction of the marshal's office?'

Buck nodded. 'I'm headed that way myself.'

'You a resident?' the man asked as the two walked away from the stable.

'No, just visiting.'

'Ah, then I'll bet you're in town to watch me work.' The man laughed before going on, 'I'm the state's official hangman. Here to carry out the sentence of one' — he hesitated a moment — 'ah . . . what's his name? Seems I should remember, don't it?'

Buck didn't answer, just kept walking.

'Clarence Handy. That's it, Clarence Handy. It doesn't seem right I can't recall someone's name when I'm gonna be the one who makes them climb the gallows steps.'

Out of the corner of his eye, Buck looked the hangman over. Somehow all he saw was black. Black riding-boots with the legs of his black-wool pants tucked into their tops, a black coat, its split tails hanging down almost to his knees. From his angle, Buck couldn't see the man's shirt, but he guessed it'd be black also. A black-felt Stetson covered most of his black hair, hair that needed a barber's attention.

Stepping up on to the wide boardwalk in front of Marshal Coleman's office, Buck waved the hangman to go on ahead. Both men stopped just inside the office door and found themselves at the back of a crowd of men, all facing the marshal who was standing behind his desk.

'I'll tell you, Marshal,' a man in front of the crowd said loud and angry sounding, 'we ain't gonna put up with it. We got our families to think about, and our stores. Having that man on the loose just won't be tolerated.'

'Now, boys, I know what you're saying,' Marshal Coleman said, sounding patient. 'But you've got nothing to worry about. Handy is still my prisoner, even if he's over at Doc Saunders's place. He's not going to be getting up out of bed anytime soon. Hell,' Coleman added, spreading his hands out in front of him, palms up, 'he's so sick he's coughing up blood. It'll be a wonder, Doc Saunders says, if he lives long enough to face the hangman.'

'Well, it just ain't right,' another man in the crowd said. 'He's been convicted and is set to hang. He should be back there in a cell, waiting for this fancy hangman the governor's got. Hell's fire, no need for anyone to be coming in to do the job, anyways. We got enough rope, don't we, boys?' he asked loudly.

'You know it, and we know how to use it, too,' one of the men standing just ahead of Buck yelled. 'No reason I can see for us to wait for any government sanctioned fool to bring in his own rope, is there? No reason at all to wait.'

'Yes, there is,' the hangman still standing beside Buck said coldly. 'The reason is that the law says only the official hangman can do the job and that's me. Now, if you want to take that away from me, then I and the marshal will have to stop you.'

Glancing down, Buck saw that the man in black had filled his hand with a long-barreled Colt. Those men nearest the hangman saw the revolver and moved out of the way, leaving a clean path to the marshal's desk.

Coleman, hearing the hangman announce himself and seeing the Colt, held up his hands, spoke up. 'There you have it, boys. The waiting is over. There isn't any reason for you to stand here complaining anymore. Go on back to your businesses and let the law do what it's got to do.'

Slowly, with some softly muttered grumbling, the crowd of townsmen, keeping one eye on the six-gun, filed from the office.

'Well,' Marshal Coleman said, falling back in his chair, 'you sure picked the right time to arrive.' Standing up, he put his hand out across the desk. 'I'm Marshal William Tell Coleman and I'm damn glad you're here.'

The hangman took the hand and introduced himself before taking one of the chairs. 'I'm George Newcomb and here,' he said, taking a folded paper from a pocket and handing it to Coleman, 'is my official documentation. Now, what's this about Mr Handy being at the doctor's?'

'Guess you don't need me,' Buck said, still standing by the open office door. 'I'll probably see you later, Marshal.' He nodded at Newcomb, then turned and walked out.

As he'd guessed, Newcomb's shirt

was black, as was the holster holding his long Colt and the belt wrapped around his waist. Thinking back, he remembered the man's horse had been a brown roan. That, he thought, didn't seem right.

7

He stopped by the hotel, where he learned that Vanessa had returned to her room but had left after changing her shirtwaist. The clerk didn't know where she'd gone. Buck figured he would find her at Doc Saunders's place, if he really wanted to see her. He didn't. He took out his pocket watch and decided it was time for a late lunch and then another glass of beer. Maybe he'd get a chance to talk with the saloon owner.

Buck took a seat in the restaurant and ordered a bowl of the ever-present stew from the big-bosomed waitress. Most restaurants served one kind of stew or another and many were even famous to one degree of another for their version. Typically, he knew, the afternoon stew was put together with whatever bits and pieces of beef or other meat that hadn't sold the day before. Remembering how Vanessa had turned her nose up at it, Buck smiled as he savored a spoonful.

After finishing his meal he sat over a second cup of coffee and thought about the way things were happening. Bringing Vanessa to French Gulch was turning out to be a little more than simply playing nursemaid. So far, from what he could see, the highlight was seeing the blonde-haired woman in the saloon. The biggest cloud on the horizon, though, would be when the hangman, Newcomb, went about doing his job. He wondered whether he'd be able to get Vanessa out of town by then.

Thinking about the long-haired saloon owner, Buck decided to enjoy a drink to settle his stomach. As he pushed through the swinging doors of the Past Time saloon, his eyes automatically scanned the stairs at the back of the long room. The stairs were empty, but standing next to Big Amos at his table against the back wall was Molly Mae. Four men were seated around the table, playing poker.

The big man had ordered a beer and was preparing to take the first sip when she came over to stand beside him at the bar. Without touching the foamy glass to his lips, he turned to find himself looking down into her blue eyes.

'Good afternoon.' Her voice was husky but somehow soft at the same time, a lot, Buck thought, like hearing an evening breeze blowing through a tall pine tree, over all strong and clear but strangely muted by the tree's limbs.

'Hello,' was all he could say.

'I'm Molly Mae and you're the big jasper riding shotgun on old Clarence's niece.'

'You seem to have figured us all out.' Buck smiled and lifted his chin toward the back of the room. 'And that's your bodyguard sitting back there, watching to make sure I behave myself.'

Molly laughed. 'Amos does take his job seriously, and at times I'm very glad he does.' She motioned to the bartender and asked for a glass of brandy.

'May I buy you a drink?'

Buck held up his beer glass. 'Thank you. Maybe after I finish this.'

'Moving Clarence out of the jail certainly upset a bunch of the local business community.'

'Now why would anyone be afraid of an old man, especially one so sick he can hardly move without coughing up blood?'

Molly Mae sipped at the dark liquor. 'They fear public opinion, I think. What would people say about French Gulch if it got around that someone sentenced to hang wasn't kept in jail? And then there's the idea that justice, whether handled legally or by self-important shopkeepers, must be seen to prevail.'

'Do I get the notion that's not your view?'

'I like the old man. He ran his shop and made some nice saddles. Far as I know, he didn't do anyone around here any harm.' She smiled and, finishing her drink, placed her hand on Buck's arm. 'But I must go do my job and talk with some of the others. Maybe we can talk again?'

He watched as she walked away, stopping at this table or that, joking with the other men. Buck picked up a new glass of beer and wandered back to stand overlooking the game being played at Amos's table. It just might be a good thing, he thought, to make sure Amos knew he was a friend. One way to do that was to sit in on a couple hands.

Over the next couple hours, Buck played his cards close, never winning or losing much. Playing cautious poker, he only bet his cards and didn't run any bluffs. Actually he was mesmerized at the flexibility of the dealer's long fingers as they sent the cards skimming across the felt. Only once, toward the later part of the evening, did anything out of the ordinary take place. That was when Amos's big right hand was suddenly filled with a short-barreled Colt.

'Friend,' Amos said softly, drawing

the pistol smoothly and laying it on the table so that it pointed directly at the man across from him, 'I'm only going to say it once. When you make your discards, make damn sure they all end up in the pile.'

The card-player, his face taking on a pasty whiteness, carefully raised both hands and placed them flat next to his cards. Slowly he stood and, not taking his eyes off those of the dealer, turned and walked away, heading for the swinging half-doors. Amos, his face not showing any emotion, slid the six-gun back into the leather.

'Cards?' he asked the other men at the table.

Buck played a few more hands before throwing in his cards and picking up his meager winnings. Nodding to the dealer, he looked around the room, but didn't see Molly Mae. Somehow while he'd been playing, she had disappeared out of the room.

He stopped on the wide hotel veranda, out of the light streaming from a window, and deftly rolled a smoke. Cupping the match, he lit it and settled back in one of the hotel's rocking-chairs. The night air was cool and pleasant after the hours he'd been breathing the stuffy, smoke-filled saloon air. Relaxed, he watched as Marshal Coleman came out of his office, locking the door behind him, and crossed over to the hotel.

'There you are,' the lawman said, dropping into another chair and putting his feet up on the handrail. 'I was just heading over to the Past Time to find you.'

'I had my meal, a drink or two and a little poker,' Buck said, pinching the fire from the end of his cigarette, 'and now it's almost time for bed.'

'Well, it isn't that late. Not too late, I hope, for you to take a little walk?'

'And where do you want to take me?'

'Oh, I'm not invited. Vanessa's been sitting with her uncle since late afternoon. I happened to run into her at dinner, over at the restaurant. She asked me to tell you, if I saw you first, that old Handy wants to see you.'

'Now why would he want to talk to me?'

'Don't know. He seems like a quiet, likeable old man, and Vanessa is getting along with him. It's going to be tough on her when that damn hangman has to do his job.'

'Yeah, I've thought of that. Guess I'll try to get her out of town about that time.'

'Sure wish there was something I could do to help her, but I'll have to be there, I suppose.'

Standing up, Buck looked down at the marshal. 'Yeah, I suppose. Guess I'll go see what the old man wants. I'll talk with you in the morning.'

Buck didn't know whether to knock on the doctor's door or just step inside. He knocked quietly in case old man Handy had fallen asleep. Doc Saunders opened the door and, smiling, motioned him to come in.

'Marshal Coleman tells me Clarence

Handy wants to talk to me. Is he awake?'

'Yep. I just left him. That niece of his has gone, says she'll be back in the morning. Now, don't you go keeping him talking very long. He needs all the rest he can get.' The doc stepped aside to let Buck open the patient's door.

'Evening, old-timer,' Buck said, walking into the room.

'Hiyah.' Handy's voice was not much more than a whisper. 'Close the door and sit close; there's a few things I wanna tell ya.'

Buck pulled a chair next to the bed and sat down. 'The marshal said you wanted to see me. What can I do for you?'

Handy was lying on his back with a thin pillow under his head. He turned to face Buck as the big man sat down. 'That girl, my Elizabeth's niece, she's been real good to me today. Getting me outa that cold cell and all. She don't know what they say I done, does she?'

'Well, I don't know what all she

might have been told, but I don't think it matters to her much.'

'Wal, I'll admit, I done a little bit of what they say I did. But you know, polishing your pants on saddle leather don't make you a rider.'

'What are you saying: that you didn't ride with Henry Plummer?'

'Naw, I never did. Hell's fire, boy, old Henry wasn't gonna have an old galoot like me around when he was doing business.' His words came slow, as if he didn't want to put too much strain on his breathing.

'All I did was hold the horses a few times. And when they'd all ride off somewheres, I'd stay back at the place to keep the fires burning. Naw, I never did ride with them. He was a good man in many ways. It was him what set me up making saddles, you know.'

'I guess that to the law that doesn't make a lot of difference, does it?'

'Nope, not a bit. Someone says that I was part of the gang, and that's all it takes. When ya wallow with pigs, ya gotta expect to get dirty. But that don't matter. That ain't what I wanna talk about.'

'And what would that be?'

'Know why I'm down here in French Gulch? I'll tell ya. Old Henry had a spread out a bit north of here. It might have been his folks' place, I don't know. Called himself Henry Plunkett when he was there. That's where we came from before we went up into the north country where he and most of the gang did their robbin' and where they was hung.'

'I never heard about him being anywhere but up there,' Buck said.

'Nope, but he was. This is where I first met up with him. I wanted to be a big, bad man. But old Henry didn't see that I could, so he let me hang around and take care of things. You know, like a horse-handler, cook and house-sitter. Him and I got to be fair good friends even. Anyhow, when he was being hung, I was known down here and had been working my saddle shop. That's what I want to ask you to do for me: go out to the place and look for something, something I want you to give to that girl, Vanessa. That's a sweet name, ain't it, Vanessa?'

'Why me and why now?'

'You 'cause she sets a lot of trust in you. And if she could spend some time out there where I use to spend most of my days, well, it might please her. I just don't really want her seeing me if this cough gets any worse.'

'What do you mean? Is that disease that bad?'

'Wal, it might be, but that ain't what changed things. You met up with that man says he's the official hangman? Let me tell you, he ain't.'

Buck frowned. 'Oh, he's the man, all right. He had the paper that said he is. Gave it to the marshal.'

'Nope, and his name ain't no George Newcomb, neither. I met old George one time. He did a hanging I was at. I'd gone up to Bannock where old Henry was sheriff. Those damn fools had elected him the year before. Anyway, I was up there taking a saddle I'd built for him and was in time for Henry Plummer's hanging. Looky here, people say when old Henry was up on the gallows about to step into hell, they say he confessed to his crimes. It ain't so,' Handy said, getting excited and lifting his head up.

'And the newspapers, they lied too. 'Give me a high drop, boys'. That's what the newspapers said were old Henry's last words. But I'm here to tell you, son, that ain't so neither.' The old man's short laugh quickly changed into a fit of coughing and he fell back in his bed, visibly exhausted.

'The one who's here calling himself a hangman,' Handy said when he stopped coughing and caught his breath, 'is a man named Cutter, Gentleman Jack Cutter is the name he was known by and I'm told it's the name that's on a bunch of wanted posters out in the gold-rush country of California. He was one of Henry's men from the beginning. Now, listen to me. He came in to talk with me, told the doc he wanted to meet me before the hangin'. All he really wanted to know is where Henry had put his hoard. Said he'd make my hangin' a lot easier if I told him. Otherwise he said he'd go after the girl.'

'What hoard?' All this talk about Newcomb not being the hangman and now something about a hidden treasure hoard struck Buck as being fanciful. It looked to the big cowboy to be the kind of tale the old man might spin to make the girl feel better.

'Henry and his boys took a lot of gold and cash before they was caught,' Handy said, his voice slowly losing strength, dropping into a raspy whisper. Buck could hardly make out the words as the old man went on, his eyes slowly drooping. 'He didn't spend much of his share, and he always got the biggest share. No, sir, he hid it. Was planning on going out to California. Quit robbing and killing and settle out there somewheres. He never made it. And the hoard is still there. That's what I want you to go get and give to the girl.'

8

Old Handy said he wasn't exactly sure where at the Plunkett ranch the hoard would be but there was one hint, he whispered. 'He always disappeared as soon as he got back from one of his trips up to the Montana Territory. Wasn't gone long. He'd say, make up some food and by the time a fresh pot of coffee was boiled he'd be back. I looked all over the place for some sign of where his hiding-hole was, but couldn't see anything.'

'And you expect me to just go there and dig it up?'

'This young lady's took good care of me, even when she knows they're gonna hang me. This is the only thing I can do for her. And you're the only one I can trust to get it to her. If anyone can, it'll be you, I reckon.'

The old man was tired. Doing

nothing all day except lie there in bed, and he was exhausted. More than likely, Buck thought, he was dreaming about there being a treasure hoard hidden off somewhere. If nothing else, this was a sure sign of how sick the old bandit was.

'All right, I'll see what I can do, old-timer,' he said, thinking it'd make the sick man feel better. 'You rest as easy as you can. Vanessa is very worried about you getting better.'

'Hell's fire,' Handy said, his voice weaker than before. 'There's no call to concern herself about me. Too late for that. Anyway, most of the stuff people worry about never happens.'

Putting the chair back against the wall, Buck stood looking down at the sick man wondering how much of what he'd said was true and how much due to a sick man's imagination. Slowly the raspy breathing calmed and became regular. Handy had fallen asleep.

Doc Saunders was relieved when Buck came out of his patient's bedroom. After checking to see how Handy was sleeping he followed the big man out on to the porch.

'When that young woman, Vanessa, sits with the old man, you can almost see an improvement in him. He rests easier. I don't think it'd be a good idea for people like you or that other fellow, the hangman, Newcomb, to be coming around. He doesn't rest easy when he's seen either of you.'

'Well, I guess he's still Marshal Coleman's prisoner so I'll mention it to him. Looks like if he says old Handy doesn't get any visitors excepting Vanessa then that's the way it is. I'll see what I can do.'

'Thanks. It'll be better for my patient.'

Walking back down the street, Buck thought about what he'd been told. Taking on the job of looking out for the girl, well, young woman, it was getting more complicated all the time. Looking up at the star-filled skies, he figured he'd better have a talk with the lawman, first thing in the morning.

'I can't see what I can do, Vanessa,'
Marshal Coleman frowned, not liking
the look on her face. The three had
met at the restaurant for breakfast the
next morning. After Buck had explained
what Handy had told him about the
man calling himself Newcomb and the
Plummer cache, they had looked to
the marshal for suggestions.

'You got to understand,' Coleman
was almost pleading, 'I don't know the
governor's official hangman no better
than you. But when someone comes
into town with the official papers, well,
I got to believe he's who he says he is.
Vanessa, look at him. You have to admit
he even looks like a hangman.'

'I wouldn't know, Marshal,' she said
stiffly. 'I've never seen a real hangman
before. Have you?' Buck caught the
coldness in her voice, calling him by his
title when a little while ago she'd been
calling him by his first name. The
marshal caught the change too.

'No, Miss Grange.' The pleading was gone as his voice became strong and determined. 'You are right in that, I've never seen the state's hangman before. I've never seen any hangman before or any hanging, either. But I did see this man's official documents, so I will believe he's what they say he is. I'm sorry, but there's nothing more I can do for you.'

The anger on her face was thick enough to cut, Buck thought, as the two men watched her carefully fold her napkin and just as carefully stand up and, without a howdy do, walk out of the restaurant, her back straight and stiff.

Left with their meal in front of them, the two men paid close attention to their fried eggs, ham slices and fried potatoes, silently finishing their breakfast. After the empty plates had been removed and their coffee cups refilled, they looked at each other and, obviously thinking about the same thing, shook their heads.

Buck was the first to speak. 'The old man said he'd been a handyman at a ranch near here before opening up his saddle shop which, according to him, was owned by Plummer. Apparently the outlaw lived there when he wasn't up north. I don't know if he was just making up a story or not. What makes me wonder is, he didn't even try to say where the gang leader's ranch had been.' Looking up at the lawman, he frowned. 'Did you ever hear anything about Plummer coming from around here?'

'No, don't think I ever heard that story. Of course I only came to this part of the Utah Territory a few years ago. There's been a lot of new people moving in since the railroad, you know, and there had been a number of ranches here before that.'

'Well, the name he used here, as Handy tells it, wasn't Plummer,' Buck said. 'The family name as was known here in this part of the Territory was Plunkett. His real name was Henry

Plunkett. To tell the truth, I'm not much interested in going out there, but the old man seems to think it'd make Miss Vanessa happy to go take a look around,' Buck said. 'I still haven't thought of a way to get her out of town . . . ' He stopped what he was saying and thought a minute. 'You know, that may be the answer. I've been wondering how to get her away from here when that hangman, Newcomb, does his job, if he really is the state's hangman. Getting her to go along with me might be the way.'

'Did I hear my name mentioned?' Neither Marshal Coleman nor Buck had seen the official hangman come into the restaurant. Looking up, they saw the man, still dressed in black, standing looking down at them.

'Good morning, gentlemen, I couldn't help overhearing part of your conversation. Marshal, I'd like to talk to you a little about what to do about Clarence Handy. Do you have a minute for me?'

'Of course, Mr Newcomb, pull up a

chair. Buck and I were just discussing how to get Handy's niece out of town when you drop the trap on Handy.'

'Well, that's probably a good idea,' he said, sitting down and motioning to the waitress for a cup of coffee. 'One of the worst parts of my job is dealing with close family members of the person about to take that final step. I purely hate the pain it can bring to the condemned man's relatives.' Turning to Buck he went on, 'I stopped by the doctor's office this morning and heard how you had a long talk with the condemned man last evening. I do hope it was in keeping with the fact that he was sentenced and will have to face his end.'

Buck, recalling Handy's telling him that this man wasn't really who he said he was, heard something else in the man's question. Glancing across the table, he saw Newcomb watching him.

'He's not a well man,' the big man answered, looking away from the hangman, 'but I think the old man has prepared himself. The fact that he's suffering healthwise is making it easier for him, I'd say. But all he talked about was how he really wasn't part of the Plummer gang, just kept riding with them to hold the horses a time or two. He claims his activities with the Plummer gang were minor, but it's enough to get him painted with the same brush.'

'He didn't talk any about the Plummer gang, did he?' Newcomb asked, sipping his black coffee. 'I mean, any thing he might tell you about the gang or the robberies could be helpful to the people they stole from. Not all the gold and jewelry they stole has been found, you know.'

Marshal Coleman nodded. 'It'd be a good thing to get that missing plunder returned to the rightful owners, all right.'

After hesitating a little and drinking more of his coffee, Newcomb nodded. 'Well, I guess he wouldn't have known much about any part of the stolen gold hidden by any of the Plummer gang, then, would he? I mean, there was some talk going on about the time those vigilantes were hanging members of the gang. Talk about how no one found much of what they'd stolen. I suppose it was just idle talk.'

Buck nodded in agreement and then, dropping a few coins on the table, pushed his chair away and stood up. 'Well, I guess I'd better go check on the young lady I'm supposed to be taking care of. See if she's over her mad turn. Gentlemen, have a good morning.'

'Here, Buck, I'll walk with you,' Coleman said, getting up. 'Mr Newcomb, I'll be in my office the rest of the morning if you need anything more from me.'

'Doubt if anything is going to happen until the old man is feeling stronger, but thanks just the same, Marshal,' the hangman said.

'Yeah, I suppose. Anyway, you know where to find me,' Marshal Coleman said, turning to follow Buck. 'You know,

Buck,' he said as he caught up just before going out the restaurant door, 'I do seem to remember hearing something about the Plunkett ranch.' He held the door for Buck.

Newcomb sat thinking about what he'd just heard.

9

Walking side by side with Buck across the dusty main street toward his office, Marshal Coleman said he couldn't recall exactly what he'd heard about the Plunkett ranch, but it was probably worthwhile talking to the old man who ran the livery stable.

'More'n likely he'd know,' Coleman said, leaving Buck to walk on down to the end of the street. Buck decided he'd better take a look at his black stud horse at the same time to make sure it was getting along.

'The Plunkett place?' the old man at the stable said when Buck asked for directions. 'Sure, and it's been empty for a few years. Or so I heard somewheres. Seems the Plunketts was a family, two, maybe three boys. Raised a few head of beef and a couple horses. Didn't come into town much, leastways

I never seen them often. The boys was big 'uns, so was their pa, as I remember. Their riding stock wasn't kept here when they did come in, just tied and then left town soon as their business was done.'

'Do you have any idea where the home place was?' Buck asked. 'I could ask old man Handy, but when I stopped by Doc Saunders' house, I was told the old man was sleeping.'

'You know that moving that old man out of the jail made a lot of people unhappy, don't ya?'

'So I've been told,' Buck said, remembering his all too brief conversation with Molly Mae. 'It don't make much sense to me, though. The old man's too sick to make it up for his own hanging. Anyway, why should the people here care about it? All the robbing and killing the gang did was farther up in the north part of the Territory.'

'Yeah, you'd think. But some of them folks down here had relations up there.

Anyway, we don't take too kindly to highwaymen, ya know.'

Buck laughed softly, 'I guess, even when the man you're talking about is too old to have done much harm. Anyway, those good people who I made unhappy will just have to work their way out of it, won't they? Now, back to my question, can you point the way to the old Plunkett place or not?'

'Wal, if'n you're thinking about buying it, I'd think again, was I you.'

'Mister, I'm the best kind of cattleman there is, one that doesn't own a single head of stock. Anyway, even if I was thinking about buying a spread it'd be a long way away from these folk. Probably back down in Texas where people treat strangers a lot better.'

The old man frowned at that and let the matter die. Unhappy with what he saw as Buck's insults, he grudgingly offered directions to the Plunketts.

'North of here, a good two days' ride, I reckon. Up along the north road that leads into the mining country.' The directions Buck was given included information about a couple smallish rivers and an old deserted mining town. 'Yah, that was what brought a lot of people out here, ya know. The strike wasn't much and nobody stayed up there long. Winters was too tough, ya know? Anyway, all that's left are a couple mine shafts that went back into the hillside a ways before all sign of gold ore petered out. I don't think the place even had a name. None I ever heard about, anyways. The Plunkett ranch is just to the west of there, about five or six miles up the creek that goes past the no-name gold strike.'

With the directions firmly in his mind, Buck went on to the corral in the back of the stable to find his big black horse looking fat and sassy.

'Having it too easy, aren't you, fella,' he muttered, breaking off a forkful of hay from a tight bale and tossing it over the top corral pole. 'Well, eat up, 'cause it looks like we'll be taking a ride.'

Walking back to the hotel, he caught

Vanessa just coming in from visiting the doctor's place. 'Good morning, Miss Grange.' Buck had been told a couple times to call her by her first name, but after the fire in her eye that he'd seen earlier, he wasn't sure what kind of response he was going to get.

'Vanessa, if you please,' she said curtly, then softened a little. 'Anyway, it's that by-the-book marshal, I'm mad at, not you.' She sighed. 'Oh, never mind, it doesn't matter.'

Buck nodded and muttered her name almost under his breath just to let her know he'd heard.

'Buck, what am I going to do? I shouldn't have lost my temper with William Tell. Do you think I should go after him and apologize?'

'I'd let him cool down a little, Vanessa. He'll be more likely easier to talk around in a couple hours.'

'We need him, don't we? Uncle Clarence and me, I mean. William Tell has been so good to us, letting Uncle Clarence stay at the doctor's place, and all. Now I've made him mad.'

Buck was afraid she was about to start crying. 'Now, let's not give up, the marshal is only doing his job as he sees it. From where I stand, he's right. Whether you accept it or not, the judge and a jury convicted Handy. Now, even if the old man didn't have anything to do with the crimes, the Plummer gang did, and, even if he was only on the outside, he was part of that gang. There isn't a lot more can be said.'

Vanessa fought back the tears she could feel coming. A proud girl, Buck saw. Not one to give up easily. The man she evetually married would have a hard time, he thought, staying out of trouble with her. Taking her elbow, he directed her up the steps to the hotel porch. He motioned to a couple wooden rockers, but she shook her head. Buck shrugged and toed one chair over nearer the porch railing and sat down, putting his big size twelve boots up on the railing.

'OK, I accept that,' she said after a

bit, dry-eyed but with a tremble in her chin. 'That doesn't mean I'm going to abandon him, though. He's still almost my uncle and he's still just a very sick old man whom nobody seems to care about. I just can't let that so-called official hangman pester him. Not if he's not who he says he is and certainly not if all he wants is for Uncle Clarence to tell him where that old gold is hidden.'

A real stubborn girl, uh — woman, Buck said to himself. 'You've been talking to that old man, haven't you? And you obviously believe what he's been saying. OK. So what can you do except what you've been doing?'

'I don't know, but I'm going to think of something.' Taking the chair next to Buck's, she sat down. 'I went over and sat with Uncle Clarence until he fell asleep. He told me he'd asked you to take me out to his old ranch. Will you? I realize Aunt Elizabeth didn't ask you to do more than keep me safe from Denver to French Gulch, but would you mind so very much showing me where Uncle Clarence worked?'

'Nope. I've been asking for directions and was coming to find you to see if you'd like to go. It's a couple days ride, you know. That means we'll have to pack soogans as well as a bait of food.'

'What are soogans?'

'That's another name for a bedroll. It's what a cowboy calls his blankets and a waterproof cover. I can get a couple from the general store, along with enough grub to last us a few days.'

Her mind no longer on her disappointment with the marshal, Vanessa nodded. 'I think it would be nice, especially if I could find something there to show Aunt Elizabeth. She's always wanted to know what happened to Uncle Clarence and why he left. I think I can explain that, but if I could find some little thing to take to her, it'd probably help her understand. Too bad there isn't any sign of his old saddle shop.'

'Well, if we got our gear together and left early in the morning, I'm told we could be at a good camping spot by dark.'

'It's too bad, though,' she said, 'that there isn't some way we could get William Tell to keep a closer eye on Uncle Clarence. Made sure that that man who calls himself Newcomb doesn't bother him.'

'Well, Doc Saunders did ask me if I could mention to the marshal that your uncle would get better quicker if he didn't have so many visitors. Guess I could pass that along to your marshal.'

'He isn't my marshal. I just . . . well . . . I just want him to go on being nice about Uncle Clarence.'

Buck tried not to let her see his smile. 'Say, how did he get a front name like William Tell? Wasn't there some hero back in olden times with that name?'

'Yes, and that's who he was named after. He says his mother was reading a book about the hero and thought it'd help her son to have a strong name like that. William Tell Coleman. That's a good name, don't you think?'

'Oh, yes, for certain. The names that a person carries can do a lot in making him what he is. Or her.'

Buck thought about the name his ma had hung on him, James Buckley Armstrong. Standing as tall as his six-foot frame would let him, he had worn the name proudly. Well, maybe not as proudly as his pa or his elder brother if having a big ranch in East Texas was the measuring-stick. Somehow the youngest Armstrong boy had never been able to keep his feet planted under one kitchen table for very long. Running the family spread was not his idea of fun. But being James Buckley Armstrong was a name to live up to, and he thought he'd been able to do that reasonably well.

Vanessa smiled at him as if she could hear the thoughts going through his mind. 'I agree, names are important. Now,' she said standing up, 'you get what we'll need for our trip and I'll go see what I have to wear. But,' she said before going inside to her room, 'don't think I've given up trying to help Uncle Clarence. I really think he's in danger and I want to help him all I can. There has to be something that can be done and maybe I can think of it.'

Buck was sure she would and he was sure he'd be involved. Shaking his head, he silently cursed Professor Fish for getting him into this.

10

It didn't take her long to come up with an idea. Buck was still sitting in his favorite rocking chair on the hotel porch thinking about whether to have a glass of beer before or after getting some lunch when Vanessa came rushing up the street. He hadn't seen her leave the hotel and had thought she was still up in her room.

'Come on, there's something I want to show you,' she said, grabbing his arm and pulling him up.

'How'd you get out of the hotel without my seeing you?'

'I went down the back stairs and out the back door. It seemed quicker than coming clear to the front of the hotel and then down the street. Come on, now.'

'What exactly is it that's got you so fired up?' he said, finding himself hurrying to keep up with her.

'I can show you better than tell you, come on.'

She led him round to the back of the stables, where he saw one horse, a tired-looking roan, already saddled, tied to the top rail of the corral. His own saddle was hanging off the rail next to it.

'Your horse wouldn't let the stableman near him so you'll have to saddle it up yourself.'

'We're going for a ride, I take it?'

'Yes. I'll explain when we get there.'

When both were in the saddle, Vanessa led the way back through the brush that filled the flats behind town. French Gulch had been founded on the banks of a small creek and had grown on both sides of it. On one side of the wide, shallow waterway, across a wooden plank bridge, was the business section. The other side was where the townspeople had built their homes. Most people didn't use the bridge but just rode their horse or buggy through the shallow water. Leaving the town from the back of the stable took a traveler away from the creek. Vanessa was taking Buck in this direction toward a low flat-topped bluff a few miles away.

Riding closer to the bluff, Buck saw they were heading for what appeared to be a sheer cliff face. Getting closer, he saw the vertical wall rise high above the flats and run for miles in either direction, broken only by tall clumps of brush that looked to have grown up against the rock-and-sandstone wall. Vanessa, leading the way, angled to one side and rode straight for one of the bigger thickets, which included a straggly stand of tall, spindly cotton-wood trees. There would have to be water somewhere close by, he knew, for the trees to grow there.

Not stopping, Vanessa kneed her roan on directly at two of the tallest trees. As he followed close behind, getting right up close to the trees, Buck saw what appeared to be a faint trail running deeper in the stand. A small creek flowed down the trail from the cliff face, spreading out and disappearing in the soft sandy flats before passing the two trees. A thicket of brush, some of the wild growth reaching taller than a mounted man, crowded against the sandstone wall behind the trees.

'How'd you find this?' he asked, ducking his head as he followed her along the brush-choked trail.

'Uncle Clarence told me about it. He said this place had been used a long time ago by road agents but he thought it had been forgotten when that gang was killed off by a posse. Come on.' She spurred the roan ahead, laughing at the look on Buck's face.

Hidden by the brush and trees, a narrow gully opened up in the cliff, worn over the centuries by the small creek that meandered from somewhere further along. Winding first one way then the other, and climbing all the way, Vanessa led the way out into the sunshine and pulled up to let Buck come beside her.

'Well, looky here,' he exclaimed softly. Coming out of the narrow ravine, they had ridden into a large opening. It covered about a dozen acres and was surrounded by steep walls of sandstone, walls that reached further up to the top of the mesa. The pocket was beautiful. Long grass covered most of it, with a few tall pines and cottonwood trees growing against the far wall. Buck figured that was where the small creek came from; probably there was a spring back there.

'Uncle Clarence said there's a cabin back in those trees. It's probably fallen in, he warned. Nobody's been back here so far as he knows since the outlaws last rode around here.'

'Well, this is something, all right. Not really big enough for anyone to make a hidden ranch, but a good place for bandits to hide. But that doesn't help us out any, does it?'

'Oh, yes it does. Don't you see? That man Cutter is after what Uncle

Clarence knows, or what he thinks he knows. Somehow he got the papers from the real Newcomb and rode in to get next to Uncle Clarence. He told Uncle Clarence that he'd hurt me if Uncle Clarence won't tell him about the gold hidden by Plummer.'

Buck frowned. 'You really believe the old man is not just daydreaming?' Buck's frown deepened. Maybe, he thought, the old cowpoke wasn't as far gone as he thought. If so, then he was in danger. Damn, so was the girl.

'And,' he said out loud, 'with the law not believing your uncle, he's got a good chance of making the old man talk.'

'Not if that Cutter fellow can't get to him, he don't.'

'What do you mean?'

Vanessa smiled, the kind of smile that Buck was getting to know meant she was going to do something sneaky. 'What you're saying is all true. So it only leaves us one thing to do, doesn't it?' Buck didn't think that was a

111

question she expected an answer for. It was, but she offered the answer herself. 'We've got to get Uncle Clarence someplace where Cutter can't get to him. Someplace where he'll be safe until you can go get Plummer's gold.'

'Wait a minute, are you thinking of helping Handy escape and bringing him back here? Hell's fire, that'd never work. Marshal Coleman's no fool, you know. Even if we could make it work, he'd know on which door to come knocking, yours and mine. No ma'am, I'm not about to put my neck in a noose.'

'Buck, it won't get to that. Look, we go back to town and buy at least a week's supplies at the store. Tell the clerk that you and I are taking a little trip. Wait until late and stop by the livery stable. Have this old horse put in the corral with your black and another horse to use as a packhorse. Later, after the stableman has bedded down for the night, you quietly get the horses, use the packhorse and get that buckboard from the livery stable and bring it around back of the doctor's house. I'll have Uncle Clarence ready. We bring him here and make him as comfortable as possible. That should be easy, all he's doing is eating soup and resting. He can do that here. We take the horses and the wagon back and sneak into our rooms at the hotel. I'll talk to William Tell later today and let him know our plans to leave early tomorrow, about sunrise. If his escape is discovered before we get away, well, we don't know anything about it.'

'Vanessa, that isn't likely to work. In the first place, your friendly marshal knows Handy is too sick to travel on his own. You and me are the only ones likely to help him. Anyway, getting the old man back here isn't that easy. How do you plan to hide the tracks left by that wagon? Coming and then going will leave marks a baby could follow.'

Vanessa's face fell. One minute she was full of excitement and then, as if he'd turned out the light, gloom clouded up and rained on her. Buck shook his head. Hell's fire, he thought, looking out over the landscape so he wouldn't see her disappointment. It was a good plan, as far as it went, and she was probably right about the danger the old-timer was in. But there wasn't much they could do about that.

Or was there? he asked himself having ridden back out of the hidden little valley and letting his eyes travel along the ground for a couple hundred yards. In either direction from the tree- and brush-blocked ravine, the creek, during the wet years, had washed out for a distance before seeping into the ground. Looking at it, Buck saw how the flood of water had left a wide sandy fan shaped stretch. Glancing left and right, he judged the distance the sand covered ground ran before thinning out into the hard pan and mesquite brush.

'You know,' he said almost to himself, 'if we brought the wagon as close to the trees as possible and I carried the old man and put him on the roan, I could get him on up into the little pocket. You would drive the wagon on a ways. See where the sand ends down there?' Vanessa, hope reborn, nodded. 'OK, I could get the old man comfortable and bring the horses back out and use a branch to wipe out the tracks, leaving those made by the wagon. We leave the wagon there and return the horses to the corral.'

'But they'll find the wagon first thing and know where Uncle Clarence is, won't they?'

'Not if they don't know about that ravine and what's up at the end of it. Most folks who have been along here never thought to look into that clump of trees. If they had, there would be more sign of it being explored. No, I think they'll spot the empty wagon and think whoever helped Handy left it and put him on a horse to make the getaway faster.'

'It'll work, Buck!' Her excitement brought a flush to her cheeks. 'I'll take the wagon on away from here and leave it where they'll see it. They'll think Uncle Clarence had help, probably from other members of that old gang. I'll get William Tell thinking about that. We can do it, Buck. If we're going to save him, we've got to do it.'

Sitting quietly, he thought it out again and nodded. 'Yeah. That's our only chance to make it work. Do you think he can ride that distance up the ravine?'

'He's tough and knowing that it's his only chance to get away from that fake hangman, I'd not worry about him,' she said, almost proud of her uncle's determination.

11

Back in town, Buck and Vanessa stopped by the general store that was only a few doors down from Doc Saunders's place, and filled a large pair of saddle-bags with as much food as they would hold. Marshal Coleman, having seen the pair ride back into town, followed them into the store.

'Looks like you two are planning a trip,' he said.

Vanessa smiled innocently up at him. 'Yes, Uncle Clarence told us about the ranch he had once worked at and asked if we'd go look it over. Seems to think there might be something there that I might take back to Aunt Elizabeth, you know, to remember him by.' Buck was open-eyed at how easily she told the story.

'How long you planning to be gone? I was hoping to invite you to a picnic one afternoon, Vanessa.'

'Well,' she glanced quickly at Buck, 'I don't know. Buck, you know about where the ranch is, don't you? How long do you think our trip will take?'

'Yeah, your uncle tried to explain it, but I talked with the old fella down at the stable. From what I was told, it's suppose to be a couple days' ride out there. Add a day or so to look around and, well that makes it about a week. On top of that, a week's supply of grub is about all we can carry. That puts a limit on things, I guess.'

'OK, then.' The lawman smiled and turned back to Vanessa. 'When you get back, we can go up the river a ways and have a little picnic.' Coleman smiled down at the young woman. 'There's a spot up there that you'll love. Lots of shade and good grass to spread a ground-cloth out on.'

Buck almost laughed. 'Is this invitation only for Vanessa?' he asked as innocently as he could. 'After all, I'm suppose to be protecting her, you know.'

Coleman smiled and shook his head. 'No, 'fraid you're not invited, Buck. Sorry. I'll be all the protection she'll need.'

Vanessa laughed and agreed to the date. 'Now, I've got to finish picking out the food we'll need. Marshal, we're leaving early so if I miss you in the morning, I'll see you when we get back.'

Coleman tipped his hat at the pair and walked back out to the street.

Following behind her as she walked down the long narrow length of the store, Buck noticed a heavily curtained window. Thinking about it, he realized that the side of the building was next to a narrow alley. While Vanessa picked up a can of tomatoes to read the label, Buck edged over against the curtain. He glanced back to the front of the store and saw that the clerk was busy talking to a woman. Carefully, he parted the curtain and, holding the basket Vanessa was slowly filling with his left hand, reached out and pulled the pins that held the bottom of framed glass in place. Vanessa didn't look around.

Buck paid for the grub and threw the saddle-bags over a shoulder, saying he'd take them down to the stable and talk to the stableman about the extra horse.

'What was that you were doing behind that curtain?' Vanessa asked before he could walk away.

'I didn't think you saw that. Well, if we're going to leave this grub for Handy, we'll get awfully hungry, won't we? I guess before I get your uncle into the wagon I'd better make another trip to the store.'

'Buck,' she exclaimed, 'that'd be stealing.'

He laughed. 'Now what do you think is going to be the worst crime, helping a man due to be hung escape or climbing through a window to finish our shopping? Don't worry,' he held up a hand, 'I expect to leave enough money on the counter to pay for what I take.'

Chuckling, he turned and walked down the street.

At the stable Buck hired a roan and another horse, one that showed a little of its Appaloosa breeding by its spotted rump.

'We'll be leaving as early as I can get the young lady outa bed,' Buck told the old man who ran the stable. 'If you don't want to be woken up, you can leave the extra saddle back with mine, in that shed out by the corral.'

The old man nodded and watched as Buck carried the horse tack and the filled saddle-bags toward the back. Next to the pole corral, the three or four wagons and buckboards rented from the stable were lined up, ready to go. Buck hoped the Appaloosa didn't mind pulling a wagon.

After enjoying a leisurely dinner, Vanessa bade Buck goodnight and went up to her room. Not expecting to get much sleep, Buck headed for the Past Time and a drink.

'Hello, cowboy,' Molly Mae greeted

him as he pushed through the doors. 'I think it's time the house bought you that brandy,' she said, motioning to the bartender.

Taking the squat bottle with the fancy label and two glasses, he followed the long-haired woman to a table near the back of the room. Looking over at the poker table, Buck saw that Amos was watching.

'I have to admit, having Amos for protection has saved me a lot of hassles, but it also has its drawbacks. He doesn't trust any man who gets near me.'

'How do you suggest I get round him?' Buck asked, pouring her drink and his own. 'I mean, if I should happen to invite you to take a ride one afternoon. There's a pretty nice place for a picnic up the river, I've heard.'

'Oh? For someone new to town, you are pretty well-informed.'

Buck laughed. 'Your marshal has his eye on the young lady I'm supposed to be looking out for. He mentioned the picnic place when inviting her to take a ride. If it's good enough for the law, it's got to be good enough for me. Now, how about it? Want to tell me how I get around that big poker-playing body-guard?'

Molly Mae's laugh was honest and made her whole face happy. 'I'll tell him you're as safe as houses,' she said after a minute. 'Are you? Safe to be with out on that little grassy spot along the river that all young men take their young women to be alone with.'

'Do the young people of this town do that?'

'Yep, and so do a couple of the older ones, and not only those who are married to each other, too,' she said, quietly. 'Or so I've heard.'

It was Buck's turn to laugh. 'Well, then I guess as soon as we get back I'll have to see about a basket of picnic food.'

'You're leaving already? After I agreed to go picnicking with you?'

'Vanessa and I are going on a little

trip up north of town. I figure we'll be back in a week or so.'

'OK. When you get back, we'll take my buggy and go for a ride. But I'll pack the picnic basket. It's certain if I leave it up to you we'll end up eating something put up by that greasy cook over at the restaurant.'

The brandy, Buck thought sipping the liquor, went down like the first deep breath of clean mountain air on a cold crisp morning. And, he warned himself, probably had the strength of a kicking mule. If he was going to be up most of the night, moving a sick old man into the mountains, he decided he'd have to watch how much of it he drank. As he was trying to figure out how to stay at the table with this beautiful woman and not get too far into the brandy, he saw Doc Saunders come into the saloon.

'There's the good doctor,' he said, thinking fast. 'He's been mighty good to Vanessa and her uncle. Do you think it'd be all right to invite him for a drink of this good stuff?'

'Of course it would,' Molly Mae smiled and started to get up. 'I'll invite him over.'

'Look, maybe there's a favor you can do me,' Buck said, reaching out to touch her arm, stopping her.

'And what would that be?' She settled back, the smile still on her lips.

'I can't tell you all about it, and it'd be better if you didn't ask. But if I pay for a bottle of this stuff, could you see that the good doctor stuck around a while to drink it? Or at least most of it?'

The woman sat and looked calmly into his eyes. 'Let me get this straight. Your Vanessa's uncle, who is sick and headed for the gallows, is over at the doctor's house and you want me to keep him here as long as I can?' She smiled, her eyes lighting up as she went on looking at Buck. 'Is there something going to happen tonight that I shouldn't ask about?'

'It's asking a lot, I know. But, well, I told Vanessa's aunt that I'd take care of her niece, and as Handy almost became her uncle and seeing as how she's, you might say, adopted him as her uncle, then' — he hesitated — 'yeah, I guess I'm just trying to help the young woman out.'

Molly Mae pursed her lips, thinking. Then, 'I never did like the idea of them hanging that old man,' she said. 'As far as I could see, all he did was make beautiful saddles which people were willing to buy. OK, no questions and I'll not notice anything happening. The good doctor will get his drink and you can pay for it when you get back.' Reaching out, she grasped his arm. 'And I'll talk to Amos. He won't like it much, so you had better make it back for that picnic or I'll send him out looking for you.'

'Oh, I'll be here. A day in your company is too good to let anything get in the way.'

Walking toward the saloon's swinging doors, Buck was feeling about as happy as he'd ever been, until he saw Doc

Saunders bellying up to the bar. Then, shaking the cobwebs from his head, he remembered what he had to do before daybreak.

12

As he turned down the alley alongside the general store Buck just touched the window to make sure it would swing open easily and silently. He glanced back over his shoulder toward the street to make sure he wasn't seen, then hurried on down the alley and down to the back of the stable.

Working in the light of the nearly full moon, Buck quickly hitched the horse with the spotted rump to the wagon. The animal moved quickly between the shafts and stood while he fit the harness over its chest. After Buck had filled the bed of the wagon with a thick layer of straw, and tossed in the saddle-bags full of grub, he saddled the other two horses and brought them to the hotel's back door. Running as silently as he could up the back stairs, he knocked gently on Vanessa's door.

'Who's there?' she called, sounding a little frightened.

'It's me, Buck. Open the door.'

He heard rustling noises and the door opened just far enough for him to see a pretty blue eye. 'Buck!' she exclaimed, opening the door wide. Wrapped in a flowered cotton robe, she started to speak, then stopped when Buck held a finger to his lips.

Whispering, he told her to get dressed for riding and to hurry. 'Come down the back stairs and don't let anyone see you,' he said before retracing his steps.

Minutes later she came through the back door. 'I thought we were going to wait until the town settled down for the night,' she said.

'We got lucky. Doc Saunders is over at the Past Time. With him out of the house, we'll be able to get Handy out without any trouble. But we got to hurry. Come on.' Without looking to see if she was with him, he quietly led the horses on down to the back of

Saunders's place.

'Hurry, now,' he said, keeping his voice low. 'Go get the old man. And bring as many blankets as you can carry.'

Buck expected it'd take a while to get Handy up and dressed and was surprised when he and Vanessa came out.

'I'd warned Uncle Clarence to be ready,' she explained as she helped Buck get the old-timer as comfortable as possible on the straw.

'I'll take it as easy as I can, Mr Handy,' Buck said quietly.

'Don't bother, just get going.'

Keeping the horses at a walk until they were away from the buildings, Buck headed toward the distant bluff, coming close a couple hundred yards from the stand of cottonwoods. Turning to travel along next to the cliff, he kept the wagon as close to the steep wall as he could. Stopping within feet of the trees, he ground-hitched the horses.

'Here's where it's going to get tough,

old-timer,' Buck warned Handy. He helped him down and eased him into the saddle Vanessa had just left.

'You do what you gotta do, young fella, and I'll take care of me.'

Turning to Vanessa, who had already climbed into the wagon seat, Buck nodded. 'Keep going in a straight line on down until you run out of the sand. Once you're into the hard pan the wagon track'll be gone. I'll catch up to you. OK?'

'Take good care of him, Buck,' she said, snapping the reins on the horse's rump.

Leading the roan, and keeping a tight rein on his black horse, Buck slowly led the way into the hidden pocket. Riding in what moonlight there was lighting up the bottom of the hidden pocket, Buck led the way to the far side. Finding the weathered and mostly fallen-in remains of the cabin took a while. Again, luck was riding with him. Buck was able to find a corner of the only standing walls that would keep the old man's bedding out of any rain shower. Buck made up a bed on a layer of pine boughs and the blankets and settled the old man as comfortably as possible.

'Now there's enough food in these saddle-bags to last you for at least five or six days. Try and keep as quiet as you can and get lots of rest. That's what the doctor had you doing back there. We'll be back to get you, I'd say, in a week at most.'

'Young man, you go on, now. But take good care of that girl. Go on, I'll be all right. Damme, I was before and I can agin. Go on with you now!'

Smiling, Buck emptied the saddle-bags and climbed back in the saddle. Still towing the roan, he gave the old man a wave and headed back down the ravine. He used a leafy branch to wipe the hoofprints out of the sand around the trees. Then, hoping he hadn't missed any, he rode on toward the waiting wagon, keeping to one side of the twin marks left behind it.

'Is Uncle Clarence OK?' Vanessa

asked when he rode up. Buck just nodded and quickly unhitched the horse from the wagon.

'Come on, let's get back to town,' he said once she was back in the saddle.

When they arrived back at the stable Buck stripped the gear off the horses and returned them to the corral. Then he walked Vanessa to the back of the hotel.

'You go on up and get to bed. I'll take care of getting our supplies. I'll see you in the morning.'

She nodded and quietly disappeared through the back door.

As he climbed through the window of the general store, Buck tried to remember the kinds of things they'd bought the first time. Then he went about filling the saddle-bags again. After leaving what he thought would be enough money next to the drawer the store clerk used, he made his way back out into the alley and down to the shed, where he stashed the saddle-bags next to his saddle.

Before going through the back door of the hotel, Buck glanced up at the moon. It had been about four or five hours since he'd left the saloon, he figured. He should still be able to get a couple hours of sleep before daybreak.

Inside, he pulled off his boots so as to be as quiet as possible and started up the stairs. He had just reached the second-floor landing and was turning down the short hall to his room when the front door burst open and a crowd of men, sounding loud and angry came piling in.

'That fella's upstairs,' Buck heard someone yell. 'Come on!'

Buck unbuckled his gunbelt and looped it over his shoulder. Then he took off his hat and spun it into the darkness of the hallway toward his room. He pulled his shirt tails out and, with his boots in one hand and his Colt in the other, he turned and stared back down the stairs.

'What the hell's going on?' he called, making his voice angry. 'I paid for a night's quiet sleep. You drunks go on about your business or by damn I'll give you something to yell about.'

'Wait a minute, Buck,' Marshal Coleman hollered from the middle of the pack. 'Don't go getting riled and start shooting. We just want to talk to you.'

'Talk! Hell's bells, it must be the middle of the night. Go on, take yourselves out of here and let people sleep. Talk can wait until the morning.'

'Now, settle down,' Coleman yelled, now in the front and half-turning to the men behind him, 'all of you. We can get what we want. There's no need to rouse everybody. This is the man we want to talk to and he's here. Come on, now. Back out on the porch. Buck,' he looked up to where the big man stood, 'you want to come down? We'd like to talk to you.'

'At this time of night? What's so important it can't wait,' Buck said, anger still cutting his words short. 'OK, if you think it's gotta be now, let's get it going. I've got a long ride to start tomorrow and I'd like to get a little more sleep.' Stomping his boots in place he followed Coleman down the stairs.

Out on the porch, with half a dozen men standing in the street facing them, Buck and the marshal stood together.

'Now, what the blazes is this all about?' Buck snarled.

'Where have you taken Handy?' one of the men in the street demanded. 'You're the one that got him out of jail, ain't you? Just so you could help him escape. We want him back. Where'd you take him?'

'Handy?' Buck asked, still letting his anger show through. 'He's over at Doc Saunders' house.'

'No, Buck,' Coleman said, watching Buck's face. 'Doc Saunders was down having a drink and when he got back he looked in on his patient only to find the bed was empty. The old man's gone.'

'Naw, he's too sick to take off.' Buck let his anger fade a little. 'That's why you let us move him. He's been getting better, but he's a long way from being able to fork a horse.'

'Don't believe him, Marshal. He's the only one it could be,' that same man bellowed.

'Mister,' Buck dropped his hand to the butt of his holstered revolver, 'you've gotten me out of bed and now you're calling me a liar. I don't like that. Are you wearing a gun? If not, better get one. Nobody calls me a liar.'

For the first time there was dead silence on the street.

'That's enough of that talk,' Marshal Coleman warned. 'You, Runkle, go about your business before you step in to something too deep to crawl out of. The rest of you, go on home. The old man's gone but there's nothing we can do tonight. Go on, I'll talk to this man and in the morning we can see better what happened.'

Slowly, grumbling to each other, the men walked off down the street.

'What a night it's been,' Coleman

said, letting his shoulders slump. Turning to Buck, he motioned to the rocking-chairs. 'Whoever helped Handy escape didn't put him on a horse. We found wagon tracks behind the Saunders' house.'

'Well, there you go, Marshal. Where in hell would I get a wagon? And where would I take him? Did you try to track the wagon?'

'That'll have to wait until daylight. Whoever it was headed straight on out into the brush. I didn't want to lose the trail, so we'll wait.'

'I've got a big black horse, Marshal, one that isn't likely ever to be pulling a wagon.'

'Someone went down to the stable just before we came up to talk to you. There aren't any wagons missing.'

For a few minutes the two men relaxed on the porch. Eventually, covering a yawn, Buck spoke.

'Well, I can't help you, Marshal. Not this late. I'm about to fall back to sleep. Vanessa and I are heading out to the

Plunkett ranch early. We can talk about this then. Now, I'm going to hit the hay.'

'Yeah, I guess there's nothing more I can do. Good night. I'll see you early.'

As he climbed back up the stairs, Buck wasn't surprised to see Vanessa, still in her robe, waiting for him.

'I heard the yelling. What happened?'

'Doc got home and found your uncle missing. Go back to bed, we can talk about it in the morning.'

She gave Buck a nod, a smile and a wave and closed the door to her room.

After picking up his hat, Buck went into his. There would be questions in the morning, but with the luck they'd had tonight, he thought it would work out. He shucked his gunbelt and boots, lay down on the bed and was instantly asleep.

13

After putting together the full saddlebags and saddling the tired-looking old roan, Buck was tying his black and the roan to the hotel hitch rail when Marshal Coleman came walking up.

'Buck, somehow I can't help but think you had something to do with Handy's disappearance. But you say you didn't so I'll let it go. That means there'll not be a chance to hold the hanging while you and Vanessa are gone, though.'

Buck looked over at the lawman and nodded. 'Marshal, Vanessa is thinking a lot about you. That means I gotta think about you too. Now don't ask any questions and don't think any bad thoughts, but believe me when I say you'll have Clarence Handy back in custody before long.'

Holding up his hand to stop

Coleman from speaking, he went on. 'And Vanessa had nothing to do with it. And the old man is safe. I felt something had to be done about keeping him that way. That fellow who's calling himself Newcomb is a bad one. No, I understand,' he interrupted the lawman before he could respond, 'you have to go by the book. I wouldn't expect anything else. Just don't get any gray hair over this. It'll all work out, one way or the other. And don't, for heaven's sake, say anything to Vanessa about it. OK?'

'No, it's not OK,' Coleman said, then thought about it and nodded. 'OK, I'll trust you. But just because of Vanessa. I guess I'll have to keep looking, though. A bunch, that same group of local self-righteous businessmen that was yelling at you last night, are getting ready to go riding after that wagon. I'll have to go along. You better hope we don't find anything.'

'Just trust me until we get back. Then I can help you protect the old man from your important business leaders and that phony hangman.'

For a minute, Coleman stood frowning. 'Yeah, I guess. Do you have any idea how long you two will be gone?'

'Well, as I've been told, it's a good two-day ride to the old Plunkett place and I expect we'll be there a day or two. I'd guess we'll be gone at least a week. The old man talked about a hidden hoard of gold and while I don't exactly believe him, we could spend a few days searching. I've got enough food in there,' he pointed with a thumb over his shoulder at the saddle-bags, 'to last at least that long. So figure another few days.'

'Yeah, OK. But make damn sure you get back. And bring Vanessa back safely too.' Coleman turned as Vanessa came down the steps from the hotel. Dressed for riding, she wore a long split skirt of supple leather, black high-top riding-boots and a white linen blouse. Her black felt hat hung down her back by its long, thin chinstrap.

'Good morning, Marshal,' she said, nodding to Buck and handing him a lined brown leather jacket, which he quickly tied behind her saddle. 'Does that brown horse understand that I'm not a very good rider?'

Marshal Coleman chuckled as he took her arm and helped her into the saddle. Watching, Buck noticed first that Vanessa was very attractive and second that the marshal was very aware of that fact. He hid his smile as he swung in to the saddle.

'Well,' he said, trying to reassure the young woman, 'we're not in any big rush, so we can take our time. That should make it a little easier for you until you get used to sitting that saddle.' He tipped his hat at the lawman and the two turned and rode north out of town.

Buck rode tall in the saddle, his erect posture making it obvious that somewhere in his thirty or so years there had been military training. The big black stud horse, after traveling behind the stagecoach and then spending the days and nights in the town corral, had been getting lazy. Even after having gone on the ride the night before, it wanted to run and Buck had work to hold it down.

They stopped for a brief break when the sun reached its highest point in the cloudless blue sky. Then they rode at a fast trot for the rest of the day. With no more than an hour or so until sundown, they reached the banks of a small river and made camp for the night. From the signs left by others, it was clear that this was a popular campsite. Cottonwood trees lined the river, making a thick border on either bank. Lush grass growing in a small meadow to one side was perfect for the hobbled horses. After a meal of pan-fried steak and sliced potatoes that had been browned in the steak drippings, they sat around while the campfire burned down before crawling into their bedrolls.

By habit, Buck had placed his bedding a short distance away from the smoldering coals, the dark shape of his body hidden from anyone in the darkness of the trees. Raising his head from the saddle used as a pillow, he could see the big black and the roan grazing in the luxurious grasses. More than once the black stud had given notice that something was not right. The animal was a better watchdog than any dog could be and several times, by a snort or a twitch of his ears, the cowboy had been warned of something he couldn't yet see or hear. Over the years, he had learned to pay attention to the big black.

A light sleeper, he was awake and had the small fire going and water heating for coffee long before Vanessa stopped her soft snoring. Breakfast was a leisurely affair: scrambled eggs that had been carried in a sealed glass jar and thick slices of ham. After rolling up their bedding and washing up the cooking pans and eating plates, they sat leaning back against their saddles and enjoyed another cup of the strong black camp coffee.

'Do you think Uncle Clarence is guilty of what they say he is?' Vanessa asked after a long silence.

'I'm not the one to answer that. From what he told me, he wasn't along on any of the raids and only held the horses when the gang stopped a stagecoach to rob. Mostly, I guess he was kept busy in other ways, taking care of the extra horses. But as a rule, he says he stayed at the Plunkett ranch as a handyman. So I don't know. Apparently a judge and the jury thought he's guilty, and I don't know as I can second-guess them.'

For a long minute she sat staring into her coffee cup. 'He's such a nice old man,' she said at last. 'It's hard to picture him robbing or killing or doing any of the things the newspapers said that gang did.'

'Yeah, I can see how you'd think that. Handy told me he left your Aunt Elizabeth 'cause he wanted to be a bad man. He wanted the excitement of it. Well, a lot of young men get that feeling, I hear. Being a husband and working in a store isn't everyone's dream and living like that can be boring. Those stories about outlaws riding free and wild has gotten more than one good man into trouble. Men and I suppose, lots of women have secret desires to go after life as if it's something that's got to be roped in a hurry before it gets away. Who's to say if they're right or wrong?'

As he got up to pick up his saddle he stopped to look down at her. 'One thing you can think about; your uncle's a proud man and I think deep down a good man. He's somewhat happy that he can look back and say, 'At least I didn't lead no humdrum life'. That's important to him, I think.'

They saddled up and rode on north. The second day was just about the same as the first, riding at a steady pace, stopping at midday for a meal and then finding a good place to camp for the night.

'According to what I was told,' Buck

said as he fixed their meal that evening, 'we should be coming to some kind of deserted bunch of buildings pretty soon. Used to be a small town that sprung up when someone found gold in a nearby creekbed. The old man at the livery back in town said the gold petered out and the town died before it got going. The Plunkett spread is off to the west a mile or two. Guess we'll be there before noon tomorrow.'

Just as the man had said, a couple hours into the morning the two rode into what had been, for a brief period anyway, a bustling little community. They stopped, sat their horses and looked over what was left of the town. The few buildings, gray weather-beaten and leaning the way the winter wind had blown them, stood on either side of the dirt street. At the opposite end, standing plumb in the middle of the trail, was a tall square structure, the white paint on the cross at the very top curling and peeling. The building behind it had collapsed. Grass and even, in a few places, clumps of low growing bushes poked up through some of the rotten timbers and planks.

'Can we stop here for a bit, Buck?' Vanessa asked, swinging out of the saddle before he answered. 'I've never been in a ghost town before. This *is* what they call ghost town, isn't it?'

'Oh, I reckon it is,' he said, going on to warn her of the dangers. 'Don't go poking around in any of those buildings, though. I don't want to have to be digging you out of one if it falls down around your ears.'

'I'll stay away from them, I promise. It's just a good excuse to get out of that saddle for a little while,' she said. She handed him the roan's reins.

He had to give it to her, Buck thought, setting back in the saddle and rolling a smoke. She hadn't complained once and he didn't see any stiffness at the end of a day's travel. The girl was a better horsewoman than she had led him to believe. The woman, he corrected himself.

He climbed down, ground-hitched the black and looped the roan's reins over his saddle horn. Neither horse would move from that spot. Sucking the acrid smoke into his lungs, he strolled over to look at one of the buildings. Open holes that once were glass windows stared blankly at him. The roof had fallen in and sunshine lit up the interior. Inside he could see the long bar running down one wall, no more than bare planks held up by empty wooden barrels, typical of most rawhide towns.

Standing looking at what was probably once the most popular place in this town, he was lost in thought when he heard Vanessa scream, the sound quickly and suddenly cut off.

Dropping his quirly, he grabbed his Colt from the holster and ran down the empty weed choked street.

'Vanessa.' His call echoed, the sound bouncing off the gnarled and eroded wooden walls of those buildings still standing. 'Vanessa, where are you?'

'She's right here, cowboy.' The voice was calm and steady, coming from his right. Buck stopped and turned and saw the girl, standing stiff and straight. Someone was behind her, his arm around her neck holding her chin up, his other hand holding a revolver pointed directly at him.

14

Silence settled in on the ghost town's deep rutted main street. A breeze, kicking up from somewhere, picked up a hatful of dust and swirled it around a bit before dropping it and disappearing. None of the three people standing like statues in the street saw the dust devil or felt the movement of air. For what seemed like a long minute, nobody moved. Then, his voice still calm and in control, the hidden man spoke.

'Now why don't you put that six-gun back in its holster, big man, so I won't have to shoot you.' For a long moment, Buck stood without moving. 'Go on, do it. If I have to I'll shoot you and then, well, you don't want to see this pretty little girl hurt, now do you?'

All of a sudden Buck knew who it was holding Vanessa. The black clothes blended into the shadow of the building they stood beside. It was the hangman old man Handy had called a fake, Gentleman Jack Cutter. Helpless, he slipped his Colt back into the holster.

'Ah, that's good. Now, unbuckle your gunbelt and kick it under that pile of lumber there.' He pointed with his Colt. Buck did as he was told. 'Now, put you hands up above your head and walk back to your horses. We'll be right behind you. Do exactly what I say and this should work out for the good.'

Buck could see the fright in Vanessa's face as he lifted his hands and turned to walk back up the street. Coming to the horses he stopped.

'Now this is where it could get tricky. I'm going to tie this little lady's hands together and I don't want you to do anything stupid. So I want you to walk out into the middle of the street and sit down. Keep your hands high,' Cutter said. From a corner of one eye, Buck could see that he now held Vanessa's hands behind her with one of his, the big six-gun was still aimed at his back.

He walked out and sat down in the dirt.

Buck watched as Cutter slipped a loop over Vanessa's wrists and then helped her into the saddle and tied her to the saddle horn. Cutter then ordered Buck to stand up, and poked his gun barrel into the big man's belly, the trigger pulled and the hammer held by his thumb. Quickly, Cutter put a loop around Buck's wrists, securing it with a tight double half-hitch.

'Now,' Cutter said. Waving Buck on, he pointed at the empty saddle. 'If you'll climb aboard we can get this little deal done.' Again, keeping Buck under the gun, he made fast the cowboy's wrists to the saddle horn.

Visibly relaxing, Cutter holstered his revolver and, taking up the two horses' reins, started walking down the street. On the far side of the pile of disintegrating weathered remains of the church, Buck saw where the man's own horse, a bay mustang, its mane and tail distinctive of the breed, had been tied.

'I wasn't sure how I was going to do

it; capture you two, I mean. I've got to thank the little lady for being so kind as to walk right up to me.' Cutter laughed as he climbed into his saddle.

'What's this all about, Cutter,' Buck asked, anger and frustration filling his voice.

'Oh, you know I ain't Newcomb, do you? Well, I figured the old man woulda told you about me. My name's Gentleman Jack Cutter,' the man said, his big smile showing teeth. 'I'll introduce you to the man who goes by the name Newcomb legally in a little while. No, and I ain't a hangman neither. I'm just a poor man looking to get a lot richer. But that can wait. Let's ride.'

Leading the way, the phony hangman rode out of the clump of falling-down buildings, heading up a gentle slope. The hillsides around the abandoned mining town had been cut bare, trees of any size used for shoring up a number of mineshafts that had been dug here and there. Looking like empty eye-sockets staring down on what had once been a hive of activity, the deserted diggings were evidence of man's lust for gold. It was that same lust, Buck thought, that was driving the man in black.

Very near the top of the grade, Cutter reined over toward a dark opening that had been cut in the bank. A tumble-down shack sat off to one side. A single post, which had probably once held up one end of a hitching rail, stood like a single sentry in front of the remains of the shack. It was to this that Cutter tied his horse.

Going first to Vanessa, he freed her bound wrists from the saddle.

'Now if you'll just step down, little lady,' Cutter said. Then keeping his Colt ready, he did the same for Buck.

'Go along into the mine,' he directed, 'but stop when I tell you. There's a pretty big hole just past the opening.'

Vanessa, walking ahead, didn't need to be told to stop. Looking down into the darkness of a vertical shaft, she shivered.

Whoever had dug the shaft had used a pulley fixed to a cross-beam to winch the earth up as he dug, following the seam of yellow mineral. Only the cross-beam was left behind when the miner had given up.

'Over there.' Cutter motioned with the gun barrel. Looking, Buck saw a long wooden ladder leaning against a tunnel wall. 'It's long enough to reach the bottom of the shaft. Why don't you pick it up, being very careful not to swing it in my direction, and drop it into the shaft.' It was an order, not a question.

Following directions, Buck slid the ladder into the dark hole. Hitting the bottom with a few feet of ladder sticking up, he judged the shaft was about twenty feet deep.

'Now, young lady, if you'll be so kind as to climb down,' Cutter said, warning her to be careful. 'I wouldn't like to have you fall,' he added.

Hesitantly, glancing first at Cutter and then at Buck, she held on to the ladder with her tied wrists and stepped down. Frightened though she was, she was determined not to let the man with the gun know it.

Again, not needing to say anything, just motion with his pistol, Cutter invited Buck to follow. Once at the bottom, Cutter quickly pulled the ladder up.

'Now, isn't that a lot better? I can stop waving this six-gun around. It was getting a mite heavy.' Cutter was out of sight from where he stood, but Buck heard him laugh.

'Here, catch,' Cutter called a few minutes later and before Buck could figure out what he meant, the saddle-bags he'd filled at the store were tossed down. Their bedrolls came next. Being busy untying their wrists, Buck didn't try to catch anything.

'I looked,' Cutter said, standing close enough to the edge of the shaft to look down at his prisoners. 'You've got enough food for quite a few days. Long enough for me to go on over to the

Plunkett spread and look around. It's only a couple miles over that way.' Again Cutter laughed. 'Oh, you can't see me, can you? Well, that's all right. If I find what old Handy was talking about then I'll come back and put the ladder down. No reason for me not to. But if I can't find it, then I'll have to come back and ask you if there's more information about where Plummer hid his gold. You'll be more ready to talk then, I reckon. Oh, you might want to feed the old man while you're down there. I didn't have anything to leave him so it's been a while since he's eaten. Probably be a mite hungry, I figure.' He turned away and Buck heard his laughter grow fainter as he walked away.

'What did he mean, Buck?' Vanessa asked, her voice revealing how close to panic she was.

'He means me,' a raspy voice said behind them, bringing a gasp from Vanessa. 'I'm back here. Too tired to welcome you as a good host would do, I'm afraid.'

As his eyes got used to the gloom from the faint sunlight that flooded the opening above them, Buck strained and could at last make out the darker mass of a man sitting with his back to one wall.

'A gentleman would stand in the presence of a lady; please forgive me,' he said. 'There's a seep back here so there's water enough, but I have yet to find one thing to eat. And I've had quite a while to search. He dumped me down here more'n three days ago. But let me introduce myself, I'm George Newcomb.'

In the faint light, neither Vanessa nor the real Newcomb could see Buck nod. He'd figured that was who it had to be. Gentleman Jack Cutter might be a thief and liar, but apparently he wasn't a killer. Not yet, anyhow.

15

Working in what light there was, Buck used wood scraps from a pile left behind by the miners to build a small fire. He heated up a meal and made sure not to overdo it. With no way to know how long they'd be down there he wanted to stretch their supplies as far as possible.

While he was doing that, and by the light thrown off by the fire, Vanessa tried to make the older man more comfortable, using a bedroll for him to lean against. She found the seep, actually a pool of cool water at the bottom of a moss-covered part of the very end of the mine diggings, and used a scarf to wipe Newcomb's face.

As far as he could see in the flickering firelight, Buck thought this George Newcomb was not a big man at all. Hard to say exactly how tall he would be when standing up, but somehow he gave the appearance of being a little less than average height. It could be, he decided, carefully turning the thick slices of bacon frying in their own grease, that he just looked like what Pa, because of his slender build, would call a 'wispy' little fellow. In the poor light the man's hair looked coal-black while his long, straggly beard appeared snow-white.

After finishing the meal, and while the fire burned down, the three sat and talked, bringing each other up to date about how they had got where they were.

'He came riding into my camp one evening,' Newcomb said, his voice sounding less hoarse. 'I invited him to share my dinner and he accepted, adding some beef to the frying pan. Over coffee, just like this, we got to talking. I was due down in French Gulch but I wanted to take a day or so to look over the ghost town. They interest me, you know.

'Well, we talked as men will around a campfire; there just seems to be something about a fire that brings that out, a willingness to share experiences. He told me he was just riding the grubline, looking for work but not in any great hurry. I explained I was employed by the government and was on my way to take care of a job. He said he knew that. That should have warned me, but it didn't, not for a few minutes at least.'

Sitting with food in his belly and his back once again supported by the rock wall, Newcomb stared into the bright-orange fireglow. 'When I looked up, trying to figure out what he meant, he had his six-gun pointed at me. He was laughing. Well, he tied my hands and feet, running the rope to a tree so I couldn't move, and after throwing my bedroll over me, went to sleep. The next morning, after fixing bacon and eggs, the last I had, he brought me up here and made me climb down that ladder he'd found. I don't know why, he never said.'

'It has to do with gold and jewels,' Vanessa said, sounding tired. 'My uncle mentioned a hoard that the outlaw, Henry Plummer had hid and that man, his name's Cutter, wants to find it. He thinks we know something about where it is.'

'Before he knew about us,' Buck went on explaining, 'he wanted your identity papers to give to the law in French Gulch so he could get next to old Handy.'

'Ah, Handy, Clarence Handy,' Newcomb said, nodding knowingly in the growing darkness. 'You might know he'd be involved.'

'But he's not,' Vanessa exclaimed, coming fully awake. 'Uncle Clarence doesn't know where Plummer hid his stolen goods.'

'Clarence Handy is your uncle? Well, I'm sorry about that, then, young lady. I truly am sorry.'

'Oh, that's not something for you to worry about. He's very sick and I doubt he'll live long enough to hang. And I don't think Cutter will let him hang, not until he's found the gold.'

'How would he stop the hanging?'

Buck chuckled. 'Marshal Coleman down in French Gulch thinks Cutter is you. Cutter had your commission and a bag of your equipment to prove who he is and the marshal accepted it.'

'I wondered why he only threw one of my saddle-bags down here and kept the other one,' Newcomb said.

Buck picked up a small twig, stuck it in the fire and when it blazed up used it to look at Vanessa. Using the rolled-up bedroll as a pillow she had gone to sleep.

Buck flipped the twig into the bed of coals and yawned. 'I guess there's nothing we can do tonight. Might as well do as she's doing and get some sleep.'

'Tomorrow won't be any different, young man. This shaft only goes back there a short way. You can see almost all of it in the daylight. There isn't anything down here except those bits and pieces of wood left behind, and none of them is more than a couple feet long. The walls are hard rock and too steep to climb. One of the first things I did was to search for anything I could use, but there are no tools with which to dig steps. I'm afraid we're trapped here until that man comes back. If he does come back, that is.'

*   *   *

Buck woke in silent darkness. It took a moment for him to remember where he was. He had helped Newcomb spread out his blankets and had used one of his to cover Vanessa before huddling in his groundsheet. The air in the shaft was cool and wouldn't heat up even after the sun rose higher.

Having never been very far underground before, he was conscious of how quiet everything was. Listening, he could hear the others breathing in the rhythm of their sleep. The sound of striking his match was loud in his ears.

Using the light, he quickly put together a few more pieces of wood to build a small fire. Carefully he stepped around the blanket-wrapped bodies, filled his coffee pot and put it on to boil. Firewood was something else they would have to ration.

He was sitting with his back to the wall, sipping coffee and inspecting the top of the shaft as the morning sun lightened things up. The shaft had been cut nearly straight down through almost solid rock. As far as he could see, the miners hadn't left enough rough spots that could be used to climb up any of the walls. The top edge of the shaft looked a lot farther away than he'd first estimated.

'Good morning, sir,' Newcomb said, keeping his voice low so not to wake Vanessa. 'I hope there's at least another cup of coffee in that pot.'

'There is. And I even have a cup, although when she wakes up one of us will have to share. How are you feeling this fine morning?'

'Ah, I slept wonderfully,' he said, accepting the hot tin cup. 'That's the first time since I was persuaded to climb down that ladder. I fear had you not come along with saddle-bags of food I might not have bothered to come out of my stupor. Have I thanked you?'

'Glad to have timed our little visit when we did.' Buck smiled.

'Yes, I don't want to think about how it might have turned out. That fellow had no need to keep me alive. He already took what he wanted from me. I have no knowledge of gold or jewels.' For a few minutes the two men sat without talking, sipping their coffee.

Joining Buck in studying the top of the shaft, Newcomb broke the silence. 'Does the Plummer treasure really exist? This is the first I've ever heard of any of that gang putting anything aside. From all the stories coming out of the Territory, what they stole they spent, either gambling or drinking.'

In the growing light, Buck studied what he could see of the framework holding up the crossbeam. 'I don't know, to tell the truth. Handy told me Plummer had plans to use some of his share of the gold they stole to make a new life somewhere, California maybe. He was kept on as a kind of handyman at the Plummer family ranch. Every time Plummer would come riding in after being up north a while, he'd disappear for an hour or so and when he returned he wouldn't have the bag he'd left with.'

'Well, this is the first I've heard of a family ranch, too. You know, from what I've heard, that Henry Plummer was a smart man. Not like most of those he ran with. It's quite possible he did hide out a grubstake, something to use to build a new life.'

Buck sat for a minute, trying to come up with an idea on how to get up and into the sunlight. 'According to Handy, the family name was Plunkett. Henry was one of two sons. Don't know anything about the other one. Handy had come west from Denver sometime back, hoping to join up with a gang and, as he said, be a bad man.' Buck chuckled. 'You know, it's funny what a man will do. Clarence Handy is really a good man, but somehow he decided that being a bad man was what he wanted. Plummer wouldn't let him ride with them more than once or twice. Handy says he held the horses on one raid, but that was all. The closest he got was keeping the Plunkett ranch in some kind of order.'

'Have you two figured out how to get us out of here?' Vanessa asked from her bundle of blankets. 'I smell coffee,' she said, poking her head out at last. Buck noticed that all signs of panic or fear were gone.

'Well, you're just in time. I happen to have an empty cup for you. And while you're getting yourself fit, I'll see about some breakfast. Then we're going to have to do some decision-making about food, fire and how to learn how to fly. Unless one of us sprouts wings, I can't think of a way to get up there.'

16

They took their time over breakfast, letting the fire burn out and sitting in the faint sunshine. Sitting as comfortably as possible in the rocky bottom of the hole, the three were unable to keep their eyes from traveling up and becoming fixed on the sunlight and the cross-beam. As the day stretched out, even that soon became no more than a dark bar across the opening.

'I feel sad, Miss Vanessa, that it is your uncle I was sent to French Gulch for,' Newcomb said at one point, reminding everyone that he was the territorial governor's official hangman.

'Yes, it isn't something I like to think about,' she said, then after a while smiled. 'Of course he's not my real uncle, you know. He was about to become my Aunt Elizabeth's husband. She's my mother's sister. Mother said they were engaged to be married but before the wedding, Clarence Handy disappeared. Aunt Elizabeth later married but I don't think she ever got over Clarence Handy. When he wrote to Aunt Elizabeth, well, I didn't have anything to do so I talked her into letting me come out West to see him. She's too ill to travel and I could see she wanted to know.'

'And,' Buck took up the story, 'I was asked to keep an eye on her. To keep her safe from road agents and other bad men. Looks like I did a good job of it, don't you think?'

'Now, Buck, you can't blame yourself. This has been a grand adventure and before it's over, I'm sure you'll figure something out.'

Buck laughed gently, 'Of course I will. That's what I'm world famous for, figuring out the impossible.'

To change the subject, Newcomb started talking about his business. 'Of course, you know I haven't always been a hangman. No sir, until I took on this work I was an undertaker back East. Just like you, miss, I wanted to go out West, to have an adventure. So I sold my business and rode the train to Denver, then bought a horse. I was going to ride the rest of the way. I didn't get far, though. A little town a couple hours ride out.'

'What happened,' Vanessa asked, expecting to hear something terrible.

'I hadn't ridden a horse enough. My, huh, my upper legs were worn and sore. I stopped at the first place that had a hotel.'

Vanessa and Buck laughed.

'That's where I met James King. While my legs were healing, he told me how he was a professional hangman. A real expert from New Orleans had taught him. Well, one thing led to another and when the Utah territorial governor advertised for a hangman, I answered the call. And here I am.'

'I never thought about it,' Vanessa said, 'I mean about being a hangman. I thought it was just someone to, you know, pull the lever on the trapdoor.'

'Ah, no, my dear. There's a lot more to the hangman's job than just dropping the trapdoor. Part of my responsibilities is inspecting the gallows for sound construction. The steps of the gallows must be in good shape and the great beam must be strong enough to handle the weight of three or more men dropping all at once. I've got to oil the hinges of the trapdoor so it didn't squeak when it drops, too. There's a lot of equipment that has to be kept in good condition.'

'That's what was in the saddle-bags that Cutter stole from you?' Buck asked.

'Yes, but he didn't get my best ropes,' the hangman said, pride in his voice.

Vanessa, slightly frightened by the talk but still interested asked what made one rope better than any other. Newcomb, anxious to share his knowledge, pulled a large leather saddle-bag around and unbuckled the three buckles. Digging around, he pulled a collection of ropes, leg-irons, and leather straps from the container until, like a magician pulling a rabbit from a hat, he took out a thick coil of black rope.

'This rope was given to me by Mr King. He used it in eleven hangings, he said.' Newcomb explained with great pride. 'It's made of the finest hemp fiber, hand-made in St Louis and treated to keep it from slipping.'

The rope he handed Buck was, he went on to say, originally just over an inch in diameter. 'It was oiled and a two-hundred-pound weight was tied to the end at which time it stretched and dried to just under an inch diameter. That's the best size for hanging,' Newcomb said. Obviously, Buck thought, a man who took great pride in his work.

'The rope is important to a good execution, but not the most important part of it all. No sir, it is using the right knot that makes a good hanging.'

Buck asked him about what made a particular knot better than any other. The other man seemed pleased to show him why he liked a certain knot. He said, 'You see, a big knot is necessary to have a humane hanging. If it doesn't break the man's neck when he drops, he strangles. That isn't a pretty sight. He just kicks and twists a lot.'

Buck heard Vanessa's gulp as she followed the talk. The big man was just about to change the topic but wasn't fast enough.

'The knot,' Newcomb, not noticing the young woman's face, went on, is put just behind the left ear in the hollow behind the jawbone. The rest of the rope is draped over the condemned person's head to hold the knot vertical so it will snap the neck when he drops. It always works for me,' he said.

Vanessa got up and hurried away, stopping at the seep to splash water on her face. Newcomb stood holding the knotted rope in his hands, looking embarassed. 'Oh dear me, I do hope . . . I apologize, miss. I fear I do get a little carried away at times.'

Buck successfully hid his smile. 'Exactly how many hangings have you done?'

For a minute Newcomb didn't answer. 'Well, to tell the truth, this was going to be my first one.'

This time Buck couldn't completely hide his laugh.

* * *

The rest of the day the three sat and watched the shadow inch along the rocky walls of the shaft as the sun moved across the opening. While Vanessa and Newcomb talked quietly about the kind of things they remembered in Denver, and the hangman described life in the cities farther east, Buck continued to try to come up with a way out.

There had to be a way, he told himself. There is always a way out of any problem, an answer. All he had to do was to find it. Darkness filled their earthen prison as only a few yards overhead, out of sight to them, the sun slowly set and stars came out.

177

17

Buck had no way to tell how long he'd slept when in the thick darkness of the mine-shaft, he came wide awake. There was a way. Maybe.

Lying back down in his blankets, he thought about it. It was right in front of him. The answer he'd been looking for, a possible way to get out of this hole in the ground and into the sunshine. Closing his eyes, he smiled as he went back to sleep. There was nothing he could do until he had daylight to work with.

Just as the previous morning, he was up and had coffee brewing before either of the others was awake. Sitting back and savoring the hot, black coffee he watched as the morning light brought the cross-beam from merely a dark shadow to an actual thing. That was their way out, if he could do it.

Careful not to waken Newcomb,

Buck took the hangman's saddle-bag and opened it. On the very top of the other tools of the hangman's trade was Newcomb's pride and joy, his best hanging rope. It was the other things that Buck wanted, though. The leg-irons and the thinner hemp rope in the bottom of the saddle-bag. He uncoiled the hemp ropes, each looking like they'd never been used for anything, and found that he had two, each about thirty feet long. Long enough, he thought, looking up at the dark shadow of the cross-beam.

As before, Buck fixed breakfast once Vanessa and Newcomb were awake. The hangman hadn't noticed his saddle-bag had been moved. While Vanessa chattered away, apparently trying to keep everybody's spirits up, Newcomb simply sat and stared into the fire. Taking the plate of food, mostly potatoes, tomatoes and other things that had been taken from the general stores' canned-food shelves, the hang-man simply sat and looked at it.

'Well, Vanessa,' Buck said, finishing his share of the meal, 'I may have come up with a way out.' He stopped to smile at her. 'The idea came to me in the middle of the night and almost kept me from getting back to sleep. Almost, but not quite.'

'What is it?' she asked, excitement bringing a big smile to her face, a smile that faded when she glanced at Newcomb. Looking at Buck, she shook her head. 'Or is this something just to keep our spirits up?'

'Nope,' he said, getting to his feet. 'But I'll need a lot of room. The two of you will have to get back out of this shaft a little.'

He picked up the leg-irons to which he had tied the end of the hemp rope and glanced up at the cross-beam. Vanessa, watching, understood and quickly helped Newcomb get clear. The hangman wasn't paying any attention to anything, going along like a child would.

After making sure the end of the rope

was lying coiled to one side, Buck shook out a few feet of rope with the leg-irons hanging free and started swinging them in a circle. Faster and faster, letting the weight of the irons gain momentum, he swung them, letting go at what he judged was the right time. The leg-irons hit the wall of the shaft just short of the top and fell back. Buck had to duck out of the way to keep from being brained by the falling weight.

'Oh,' Buck heard Vanessa say as he coiled the rope again and started swinging the irons round and round once more.

Time after time, stopping only when his arm gave out, Buck tried, sending the irons up only to have them fall back. Only once did they strike the crossbeam. All through the morning, or what Buck figured was the morning, he swung the iron weights round and round before letting go, and watching as they traveled up, bounced against the wall and fell back down. Eventually, while resting his arm, he sat back and thought about what he was trying to do. It was the only answer he could come up with, so he'd just have to keep trying.

Newcomb offered to swing the rope one time when Buck's shoulder gave out and he had to stop. Once even Vanessa asked if he thought she could do it. In both cases, Buck smiled and after a rest went back to swinging the rope round and round.

When at last the leg-irons sailed up past the beam and dropped down the other side, all Buck could do was stare at it. His right arm hung loose at his side. He'd almost given up and had reached the point of believing it would never work. But there the irons were, hanging a few feet over his head, the hemp rope hanging down both sides of the crossbeam. For a long minute he just stood and looked at it.

Buck knew he was the only one capable of climbing the rope, but until he got some strength back in his right arm they were no closer to getting out than before. Vanessa started the fire and made coffee while he sat against the wall and massaged his shoulder. A good night's sleep under the stars would, he thought, make all the difference, but there was still work to do before that could happen.

He ate the meal Vanessa prepared using up the last of the bacon and the rest of the bakery bread. Then Buck sat and rested as long as he could. At last, unable to sit and stare up at the beam any longer, he got up and, taking the doubled hemp rope in his big callused hands, he started to climb. Hand over hand, wrapping the rope round his booted feet, he pulled himself up. Quickly he discovered the calluses that toughened the palms of his hands weren't enough. The rope was cutting through them and his grip was starting to weaken by the time he was able to reach an arm over the beam. For a long minute he let his body hang while he tried to catch his breath. He couldn't remember breathing at any time during his climb.

Using his arms he swung his body up until he could sit on the beam. Little by little he inched himself along, until he could jump down and stand beside the mine's opening. Full sunlight warmed him. From the angle of the sun the day wasn't as far gone as he'd thought it was.

Buck swung the ladder down. Vanessa and Newcomb, his saddle-bag of ropes and equipment hanging from his shoulder, came hurrying up. As they stood beside Buck in the full light of day they broke out laughing.

'I never thought I'd ever get out of there,' Newcomb said at last. 'I'm embarrassed to admit it, but I had given up all hope until you two came down to join me. And even then . . . ' He let the words taper off. Buck gave his hands a close inspection, then looked up at the man. For the first time he could clearly see the real hangman. In the gloom of the shaft it hadn't been clear what kind of man Newcomb was. Now he could see him to be a short, thin man, standing not much taller than Vanessa. His eyes looked dark from where Buck stood, as black as the close-cropped hair on his head. The bottom of his face was covered with a shaggy full beard. After being in the dark hole as long as he had, his clothes were caked with dirt. Only his shirt, which had once been white, was halfway clean, especially where the twin bands of his suspenders had protected the cloth.

'Well, we're out and now we got to make sure we stay out.'

'What should we do, Buck?' Vanessa, looking tired and stressed, asked quietly. After facing the hopelessness of being abandoned in the mine shaft, she was exhausted to find herself alive and well. Dirty and straggly hair and all.

Buck thought a minute and then walked over to the falling-down shack. He kicked open what was left of the door and saw a pile of saddles. Cutter had no use for the gear and had simply tossed everything in there, out of sight. He'd probably let the horses run, thinking that sooner or later someone would catch them and that'd be the finder's lucky day. Shaking his head in disgust, Buck reached in and brought out his saddle and bridle. He removed the lariat from the saddle and shoved the hulk back in the darkness of the shack.

'I don't imagine my black is far away. He probably didn't like being unsaddled and I know the stud horse is mean enough not to let Cutter put a rope on him. If there's water in the area, I'll bet that's where my horse is. And maybe even your roan, Vanessa.'

'Well, I'm not sure exactly where it is from here,' Newcomb said, 'but I rode past a small pond just before reaching that deserted mining town. I was planning on camping there for a few days.'

'I guess I'll go see if I can find it, then,' said Buck. 'It'd probably be a good idea if you two didn't just hang around out here in the open. Cutter did say something about coming back if he didn't find anything at the Plunkett ranch.' Looking around the hillside, he spotted another mine opening further along, just below the top of the ridge.

'Why don't you both head over there? Stay in out of the sun, out of sight as much as you can. Don't start a fire, in case he does come back. I'll find something to ride and we can plan on what to do then.'

Leaving the two, and keeping a lookout as he went, Buck started down the hill, back toward the ghost town. It took him about an hour to find the pond Newcomb had mentioned. Standing in a small meadow at the far end was the black stud horse. Farther in the shadows of a stand of pine trees, the roan and another horse were calmly chomping at the grass.

'Hey, you black devil,' Buck called. 'You've got work to do.'

Walking around the edge of the small lake, he was able to come right up to the horse. He held out a hand as if he had something in it. The big black stuck his nose out and let Buck fit the bridle in place. Buck used a huge rock to climb bareback on to the black, and looked at the other two horses. One must be the hangman's, he figured. Rubbing his sore shoulder, he thought about swinging a loop over their heads. That would just have to wait a while. He had something else to do before going back up the ridge.

Riding down the deserted street, he stopped at one place and slid off the back of his horse. Careful not to stick his hand into a sleeping rattlesnake, Buck reached under a pile of disintegrating lumber and pulled out his belted six-gun. After cinching it around his waist and letting it settle in place, he pulled the big Colt and checked the loads, filling the chamber he normally left empty under the hammer with a bullet from the belt.

'Now, let that damn lying hangman come calling,' he said, making sure the thong was tight over the pistol's hammer.

Back at the pond, he quickly roped the roan and the other animal and, after tying them nose to tail, headed back up to the top of the ridge. He stopped at the shack and saddled both horses before riding on to the mine where Vanessa and Newcomb were hiding. Now he had to think about what to do next. Sending Newcomb and Vanessa back to French Gulch might be the best thing, but that could also put Handy a step closer to the real hangman. On the other hand, Buck couldn't see letting Cutter get away. Something would have to be done about him, but not if it put Vanessa in danger.

As he rode to the other dark mine opening, he made his decision. Vanessa wouldn't like it, but that was the way it would have to be.

18

It turned out he was right, Vanessa didn't like the idea of her riding with Newcomb back to French Gulch.

'It looks like the only way I can be sure you're safe, Miss Grange,' he argued, using her last name, hoping she'd get angry. 'I won't feel safe from Cutter, not knowing where he is or what he's doing. We can't be looking over our shoulders all the time, expecting him to come riding up. All we've got is one six-gun between us and it only makes sense for me to ride on to the Plunkett spread. If I've got to watch out for you two then I won't be able to concentrate on catching him out. Surely you can see that, can't you?'

'No, Mr Armstrong,' she shot back, not letting her anger put her off, 'I can't see that at all.' Neither of them heard Newcomb's weak attempt to interrupt.

'In the first place,' she went on adamantly, 'we don't have enough food left as it is. Leaving you enough to ride on and then follow us back, there just isn't enough. But that's not the only thing. I'm the only one who knows where to find what Uncle Clarence sent us looking for.'

That news stopped Buck in his tracks. 'What? You mean that old man really had found where Plummer, or whatever his name was, had hid his treasure? And he told you?'

'He said he didn't completely trust that you'd bring it back. Buck, you can see that, can't you? Uncle Clarence wanted it for me and Aunt Elizabeth. Apparently there isn't all that much left. He said he'd gotten into it a couple times, to take enough to set up his saddle shop, mainly. He thought of it as simply drawing his wages.'

'Hell's fire,' Buck spat to one side in disgust. Without thinking he massaged his right upper arm. Swinging that blasted iron weight had left it a little stiff and sore. 'That old man couldn't tell a straight story if he had too. OK, then. You tell me where the gold is . . . ' He stopped when Vanessa shook her head. Exhaling through his nose in irritation, he tried again. 'Well, how about if you two just stay here. I'll go looking for him. Once it's safe, then I'll come back and get you.'

Once again she didn't say anything, but shook her head. 'Damn it, girl,' he said, raising his voice in frustration. 'I can't be protecting you and watching out for Cutter at the same time.'

When the two stopped thinking of new arguments, Newcomb spoke up. 'What, exactly, do you plan on doing to make it safe for us? Are you going to simply shoot him?'

Buck plainly hadn't thought much about that. 'I don't know. That will have to be left up to Cutter, won't it? I suppose you have a better idea?'

'No, but I can see how having us along would cause you problems.' Turning to Vanessa he put his hands out, pleadingly. 'There's enough food, that's not the problem. It's simply that he's right. He can't be worrying about keeping you safe and at the same time dealing with Cutter. I agree with him: the best thing is for us to leave him here and ride on toward French Gulch.'

Rubbing the roan's nose, Vanessa frowned as she thought about what the little man had said. At last she nodded. 'I guess you're right. OK, Buck. Saddle the horses and we'll head back toward town. But you have to promise you'll be careful. I don't want to have to deal with bringing Uncle Clarence back to town by myself.'

Buck tied the near-empty saddle-bag on to the back of the roan and helped her into the saddle.

'Buck, Uncle Clarence said there's a rock cairn near the top of a small hill up behind the main ranch house. Up beyond that you'll see a huge old oak tree that forks into two main branches. If you sit your saddle, you can see a big hole in the main trunk where the branches meet. What Plummer left is in a metal box in that hole. Uncle Clarence didn't trust you, but I do.'

'Dammit girl, with that kind of trust what else could a man do, but bring it all back to you? Go on, now. We've wasted enough time arguing. Don't ride the horses too hard and you should be back in town by dark tomorrow.' Turning to Newcomb, he went on, 'You take care of her, or I'll use that hang rope you're so proud of on you, understand me?'

'No need to threaten me, she'll be all right.'

He watched as they rode down the hill and out of sight. Now all he had to do was find the Plunkett ranch without running into Gentleman Jack Cutter.

★ ★ ★

The ranch was just where he'd been told it was. What had once been a wagon road running parallel with a swift-running stream was now just a wide swath of grass and weeds.

Riding toward the afternoon sun, he followed the small stream, slowly gaining in elevation as he rode into the foothills. As he topped a low-lying ridge he pulled up. Farther on in the distance he could see the dark purple of a mountain range. Being a cautious man, and not knowing exactly what he was riding into, he made it a habit to take his time before riding out into any clearing or topping any of the low ridges. Depending on how patient a man Cutter was, he could be coming back to ask more questions about Plummer's stashed hoard. It would be far better, Buck knew, for him to see the man in black before the man in black saw him.

There was still enough daylight to make out the ranch house and the few outbuildings still standing when Buck again reined in the black. Sitting the saddle quietly at the edge of a clearing, he took his time to give what was left of the mostly fallen-in buildings a careful once-over. The black stud horse stood quietly, head down as it pulled at the dried grasses while its rider studied the layout. As the sun went down behind the hills farther on, Buck moved back into the cover of a stand of pine trees, where he hobbled the black horse.

Before full dark settled in, when he would take up his stand again, he sat with his back to one of the larger trees, waiting and watching. Nothing moved. There was no sign of Cutter or his horse. The moon that had given him light enough to get old man Handy settled in had disappeared in its cycle. With darkness the sky exploded in a myriad of stars poking through the black velvet of the night.

Once there was the sound of the black horse making a soft snort and a few seconds later a big, full-antlered buck deer came silently through the trees a few yards away. Then, probably catching the scent of a tired cowboy who had been in the same clothes far too long, the deer made a startled woofing noise and disappeared in a single jump.

The soft breeze that had sprung up at sunset, in the beginning no more than a slightly felt movement of air, had grown until it could be heard rustling through the pine boughs overhead. Relaxed, Buck let his mind wander. Then, fighting to keep his eyes from closing, and thinking about rolling a cigarette before dozing off, his head came up almost with a snap. He'd been almost asleep; the smell of smoke brought him wide awake.

Standing up with his back to the tree so he wouldn't be highlighted against the starlit sky, Buck slowly let his eyes wander. At last, out of the corner of one eye, he saw a faint indistinct glow in the dark. Looking directly at the spot, all he saw was blackness, but holding his gaze to one side he was able to barely make out a pale haze. Cutter was enjoying a fire. Probably even a hot cup of coffee to go with his meal. The thought brought a soft rumble from Buck's stomach.

Buck realized that it would be impossible to sneak up on the man and his fire. In the darkness he'd be sure to make enough noise to wake the dead. He would have to wait until sun-up. Just knowing the man was there would have to be enough for now. Knowing where the enemy was and not announcing his own presence was, he recalled from his days in the army, the best first step to winning the battle.

Slowly and as silently as he could, he made his way back to his horse and, keeping a tight hold on the reins, retreated back the way he'd come. Finding a small clearing, and moving by feel and long practice, he hobbled the black and spread his bedroll. He'd do battle in the morning, rested but hungry.

19

Buck Armstrong was brought out of his sleep by a dull ache in the muscle of his right shoulder. A couple times during the night, when he'd been lying on that side too long, he'd come partly awake, only to roll over and go back to sleep. This morning, with the sun just about to pop over the trees to the east, the ache was less, until he began rolling his soogan. A stiff shoulder wasn't something he wanted to get into a gun battle with.

Wiping the morning dew off the big black horse helped warm him up and even seemed to loosen his shoulder a bit. Before climbing on to the back of the horse, he thumbed the thong from the six-gun's hammer and, after ejecting all the shells, tried a quick draw. Nothing to brag about, he knew. Slow and, what was worse, jerky.

Trying not to think about his grumbling stomach, he stretched, trying to extend his right arm and shoulder as far as he could. He slipped the unloaded revolver back into the holster, and stood for an instant. Then, moving as smoothly as possible, he drew, snapping the hammer at the top of his draw. Anyone who knew anything about pistols and getting them into action fast knew it wasn't always the first gun drawn that scored the most hits. All too often, and he had proved it to himself more than once, it paid off to make that first shot count. Getting your sixer out first would help, no question. But it rarely counted for anything if your first shot went into the dirt.

Working his arms and shoulders, he walked around the little grassy opening that had been his bedroom. Somewhere over that way, probably having already searched through the buildings, Cutter would be trying to find some sign of a hidden pot of gold. The trick, Buck thought, was going to be to not let the bad man see him coming. That meant he couldn't just ride in. It would be a lot safer to circle around a bit and come in after he saw where the man was. Rule number two learned on the battle ground during the Great War was to pick the place of encounter.

If he was lucky, he thought smiling thinly, he could get Cutter under the gun and there wouldn't be any shooting. It'd suit him fine to take the man back to French Gulch as a captive. Marshal Coleman would have to believe what Cutter had done when all three told the same story.

Leaving the black horse hobbled in the clearing, Buck hiked back to about where he had been the evening before. The deserted ranch buildings were off to his left, standing silent and still. Whoever had built the ranch house had placed it in a wide bowl that opened up toward the lower part of the range. The buildings were backed up to the forest, the trees protecting them from any northern wind. Cutter's fire had been somewhere in those trees, up above the house and barns. With the morning sun to his right, Buck saw that if he stayed in the trees that covered the ridge he would be out of sight from anyone near the ranch. After checking his horse's hobbles, he started out.

High-heeled boots were perfect for keeping a rider's feet securely in the stirrups, but they were not built for walking, especially through the forest. Not knowing how far to circle, once directly above the ranch buildings Buck started angling up the hillside. Somewhere in this direction, Handy had told Vanessa, there was a rock cairn and a big oak tree. Taking his time, both because of his aching feet and keeping in mind that Cutter was likely close by, he continued on.

It was the smell of smoke that stopped him. The early morning breeze he'd felt back in the clearing had died. There was no way of telling from where the smell was coming. All he could do, he thought, was slowly circle around.

Before he could move, he heard a horse's snort directly ahead. Crouching, he slowly and quietly moved forward, going from one huge pine tree to the next, stopping in his tracks when he spotted a quick movement. Slowly, with his six-gun in hand and keeping behind a huge tree trunk, he stood up. Cutter's brown mustang was standing hip-shot in a sunny patch of forest. Off to one side a rock fire ring held smoldering chunks of wood. There was no sign of Cutter.

Backing away so not to spook the dozing horse, Buck continued circling around until he was above the hidden camp. On the ridge top he came to the forest's edge. At some time in the distant past a forest fire had cleared off the trees, leaving an opening. Directly in front of him was what had to be the oak tree that Handy had told Vanessa about. A short way down the hill, Cutter, his back to Buck, worked at tearing down a pile of rocks.

For a few minutes Buck watched as

the man pulled rocks away, tossing them down the hill. He had removed his black suit and was wearing faded jeans and a cotton shirt that had once been brightly colored but was now sun-bleached to gray. A heavy holstered Colt sagged the gunbelt around the man's waist.

Feeling a warming twinge in his right shoulder, Buck decided not to let the working man have even that much edge. He drew his own revolver and holding it down along his pants leg, stepped out into the morning sunshine.

'Hey, Cutter,' he called softly. 'Find anything?'

For an instant Cutter froze, and then faster than Buck believed possible, the man jumped to the other side of the pile of rocks, pulling his Colt and firing. Buck was caught flat-footed.

20

As he threw himself to the left Buck heard bullets thudding into the oak tree. Rolling over before raising up enough to return fire, he felt the big revolver buck in his fist. Not waiting to see where his shots had gone, he scrambled round behind the tree.

'Damn you,' Cutter yelled. 'How in hell did you get out of that pit I left you in?' Silence dropped over the hillside like a thick blanket. Then, sounding almost happy, he called again. 'You are a piece of work, boy. Sneaking up on me like that. Now, what say we put up our guns and talk this over? I expect there's enough of old Henry's cache to satisfy us both. There isn't any need, far as I can see, to be shooting each other, now is there?'

Buck levered the spent shells from his Colt and thumbed in new ones. 'Nope,' he called, 'and the fact that you left that old man and the girl and me to die down in that hole in the ground, well, I don't hold that against you at all.'

Cutter laughed. 'Oh, well, I did plan on coming back. After I found what I was looking for. You probably don't believe me, but I was going to.'

'Uh huh. Sure. How is it that you've had . . . what . . . two days to search? What have you found, other than that rock cairn?'

'Not much, I'll admit. All this pile of rocks is, is a property boundary. I'm beginning to wonder whether Plummer really did hide anything. You talked with the old man; do you think he could have been pulling your leg about it?'

Buck listened and thought there was a change in what he heard. 'Oh, I think he was telling the truth,' he said, then he stopped, hoping that Cutter would say something.

Cutter didn't for a minute or two, then he had to ask, 'Well, what did he say? I mean it when I say if there's anything, there's enough for both of us. Hell, man, I'm not greedy.'

Cutter's voice was different. He was moving away from the rock pile. Quickly, without thinking about it, Buck dropped to his belly and started crawling away from the open area. He dropped down into a small fold in the ground and, staying crouched over, he ran back the way he had come, toward Cutter's camp. No matter what, sooner or later the man would have to come get his horse.

*   *   *

The bay horse stomped and its head came up, warning Buck that Cutter was close by. He had found a place from where he could see the entire campsite. The mustang was directly across the little opening from him. Silently, almost as quiet as the buck deer the night before, Cutter came round to stand by a pine tree, hesitating while he studied the forest around his camp. Eventually, reassured by the horse's reaction, he stepped out. He was bending to pick up his saddle and bridle when Buck thumbed back the hammer of his Colt.

He had waited until Cutter had both hands on the saddle and was just standing up when he made his move. The loud mechanical click seemed to echo in the forest stillness.

'Damn, but you're a tricky one,' Cutter said, looking around at Buck. Without another word, he dropped the saddle with his right hand and, swinging it with his left to catch Buck's attention, drew his revolver and fired.

Buck saw the flame flare out of the barrel and heard the noise of the gunshot, but at the first movement he had simply brought up his own Colt and touched the trigger, shooting from the waist. Both men's guns went off the same time, the noise blending into one. Neither fired a second time. Cutter's body lurched as the .44 caliber bullet drove into his chest. For a brief second he simply stood there, staring at Buck before, eyes already glazing, he crumbled. Buck glanced from the fallen man to the gouge in the forest floor left by Cutter's shot.

* ★ *

The mustang hadn't liked having the dead man's body draped over its back. Probably, Buck thought, it was the smell of blood that upset it. But he was eventually able to rope the body down for the short trip back up to the rock cairn. There was no reason that he could see to haul Cutter all the way back to French Gulch. Better to simply bury him here and tell Marshal Coleman where he was. If anyone wanted to move the body, well, that'd be up to them.

The handle of the shovel Cutter had been using while digging holes around the barn and the ranch house had been broken in half, but was still long enough for Buck to use. Digging a deep enough hole in the hillside was easy, the soil was thick loam. All the rocks that had been used to build the cairn, and which were now covering the grave, had to have been brought from someplace else.

After placing the last of the rocks on the mound, Buck had climbed bareback on to the mustang and, sitting close up to the big oak, saw the hole that Handy had said was there. Not giving any thought to what kind of beast might be sleeping in the black hole, he reached in and felt around. He cursed when he tore a fingernail trying to get a hold of the smooth tin box he found, but after long moments he pulled it free.

The box looked to have once been used to hold soda crackers; the bright colors painted on the outside had been scratched and had faded to nothing in places. A simple hasp kept the lid tightly closed. Two cloth sacks, both looking rotten, were all that was in the box. One sack fell apart when he picked it up, letting loose a flood of gold coins. Picking one up, Buck saw it was a $10

Liberty coin, minted in 1847. The other bag was stronger and didn't tear. He pulled the drawstrings and saw it was filled with jewelry, necklaces, rings and at least one large closed-case pocket watch.

If these were the takings from Plummer's life of crime, it seemed to Buck to be a small amount to trade for the many lives it had cost.

Back at Cutter's camp, Buck found the man's saddlebags and enough food to make a few good meals. Kicking the still smoldering coals from the breakfast fire into shape, he quickly boiled coffee before cutting strips of ham from a large chunk. Tearing pieces of hard, dry bread, he swabbed up the juices from the fry pan and enjoyed the first meal in far too long.

He filled one of the dead man's wool socks with the gold coins and placed the jewelry in another. Then he put both bags in the bottom of the saddle-bags. After tying them on to the back of Cutter's saddle, he rode the mustang back to where the black stud horse was hobbled. The black didn't pay any attention to the smaller brown horse as they headed back toward the dilapidated mining town. Buck decided not to push it, going back to French Gulch, but thinking about old man Handy still hidden in the little pocket outside of town changed his mind. He had two horses to ride; by changing from one to the other, he could be back in town before dark the next day.

Kicking the black into a trot he left the mining area and its memories behind.

21

The ride south was uneventful. Pushing both horses throughout the rest of the day, Buck rode steadily, making camp just as the sun was going down. Stopping at the camping place by the river only long enough to water the horses, he had continued riding. He found a spot a short distance from the main trail, next to a small stream further on, and there he made his night camp.

Up before daylight, he quickly cooked what was left of Cutter's supplies, taking a few extra minutes over the last of the coffee before hitting the trail again.

Taking pleasure in the cool morning air, he leaned against his saddle and sipped the strong black coffee as the morning mist slowly dissolved and the sun's light grew brighter. An owl, making one last silent pass over the wild grasses that grew in the forest opening, disappeared into the trees. A faint squeak some distance away told of the owl's success. As the early-morning light grew, shadows from the tall trees became more distinct. Mixed with the pungent smell of the dying camp-fire was the fresh odor from the forest growth. Without a doubt, Buck thought, this was the best time of day. He hoped old man Handy had been able to enjoy his mornings in the tiny hidden valley.

He saddled the horses, carefully piled dirt on what was left of his morning fire and headed out. Throughout the day he rode, not stopping except to water the horses, changing from one saddle to the other so as not to overwork either animal.

When, off in the distance, he spotted the long, low, flat-topped butte, he angled off the wagon trail in that direction. The sun was well past the highest point of its day-long journey when he rode on to the section of sand that had been washed out of the small concealed ravine. In the few days since they had driven the stable's wagon along that stretch, there had been enough wind to almost erase the tracks the wheels had gouged. Only in one or two places could Buck see the sign left by the searchers' horses. There was no indication at the stand of cottonwood trees that anyone had seen anything to warrant closer investigation.

Leading the mustang into the narrow ravine, Buck made quick work of it, coming out into the pocket. There was no sign of anyone having been there until he rode closer to what once had been the cabin. Little had changed, he saw. The old man was wrapped in his blankets, sitting up with his back to one of the remaining cabin walls.

'So, you didn't ferget me after all,' Handy said, sounding as strong as Buck had ever heard him. 'I sorta figured you'd be coming around today or tomorrow. Didn't think it'd take you long to get out there and back. Did you find the stuff?'

'Yep, it was right where you told Vanessa it was.' Buck said, climbing out of the saddle and stretching his muscles.

'She told you, huh? Well, it weren't that I didn't trust you, exactly,' the old man started to explain, then he stopped.

'No,' Buck cut in, 'it was just that you didn't trust me. But yes, she told me and I found it. It's all in the saddlebags on that mustang there.' He pointed at the brown horse. 'How've you been making it? Have any problems?'

'Naw, just lying here listening to the wind blow,' the old man said. Buck noticed his breathing seemed to be a little easier and that he wasn't coughing. 'Actually, it's been pretty nice, being here. Better than where you found me, in that damn jail cell. How's Miss Vanessa?'

'Oh, I expect she's fine. She rode back a day or so ago.' Buck stopped and then went on to explain briefly about running into Cutter, ending by assuring the old man that he was no longer in any danger from the phony hangman. 'But Cutter won't be coming around to bother anyone any more,' he said, finishing the story.

'Left him there, did you? I hope you put him deep. Don't care if the coyotes get him, but wouldn't want anyone bringing him in.'

'I don't think anyone will be digging him up. I put him under the rock cairn, up by the big oak tree.'

Handy seemed to like that. 'Serves him right, making him part of that old boundary marker.'

'Of course,' Buck said, 'the bad news is that the real hangman is now in French Gulch.'

'Well,' Handy said after a minute, 'I expect it's about time I paid for what sins I committed. Can't hold that against anyone.' Handy looked up at the sky. 'There's still enough time to get me back to town. It wouldn't do Miss

Vanessa or you any good to have people think about your helping me escape, now would it.'

'No, I told the marshal that you'd be back. Think you're in good enough shape to ride back? We could wait until the morning and I go get that wagon again.'

'Naw. Hell's bells, I been forking a saddle nearly all my life. If'n we don't got to run any races, I figure I can keep up with you.'

Rolling up the blankets and ground cover, Buck tied it all on over the saddle-bags on the mustang. It was when he picked up the grub sack he'd left with Handy that he saw how little the old man had been eating.

'What happened, you lost your appetite?' he asked, hefting the sack. 'There's almost as much here as I brought.'

'Well, I guess I just wasn't hungry. Don't matter. Come on, let's get riding. I want to see Miss Vanessa.'

Helping the old man into the saddle,

he watched as his gnarled hands locked on to the saddle horn. Again leading the mustang, he led the way down the trail and away from the stand of trees.

'Hey, there,' Handy called, his voice coming weakly. Buck pulled the black to a stop and turned back to the old man.

'You OK?'

'Yeah. I was just thinking. What are you gonna do with Plummer's hoard of stuff?'

Buck had been giving that some thought. 'I guess that's for you to decide. As I recall, you wanted that for Vanessa, didn't you?'

'Yeah, but she might not think it fitting, being stolen and all.' For a moment the old man didn't say anything, just sat back taking deep rattling breaths. 'You've done good, young fella, and I appreciate it,' he said at last. 'How about if you take care of it for me? Figure out a way to get her to take it.'

Buck chuckled. 'First you didn't trust

me and now you do?'

'Wal, I guess I'll have to, won't I. It's too late for me to do anything with it. You do it, will you?'

'OK, but I'm not sure I like it much.'

Nothing more was said as they rode back through the brush toward town. Buck held the horses to a slow walk, not wanting to jar the old man too much.

Coming within sight of the outbuildings, Buck reined the black toward the back of Doc Saunders's house. He ground-hitched the black and helped Handy off the mustang. Then, holding him upright, he knocked on the back door.

'OK, OK, quit your banging, I'm coming,' someone called from the inside. 'What you doing, coming in the back, anyway?' Saunders was complaining as he swung open the door. Seeing Handy, he stopped protesting and reached out to help Buck. By the time they got the old man into the front bedroom they were nearly carrying him.

'You've got your nerve, young man,'

Saunders observed, as they quickly stripped the boots and pants off Handy. Getting him under the covers, he took the thin bony wrist in one hand, checking his pulse. 'Removing him like you did could've killed him, you know. This is a very sick old man. It's a wonder he's still breathing.'

'Doc, he thought he was in greater danger here, and I agreed with him.'

'Well, what changed? Now he's a lot weaker and so you bring him back to die?'

'The danger he was in has been taken care of. He'll be better off here, now.'

'I'll say. Go on, get out of here. This time nobody's going to bother him.' Waving Buck away, the doctor carefully tucked the blankets around Handy. 'We'll just see what the marshal has to say about this. And the good people of French Gulch. They weren't too happy about Handy escaping, you know. He's too sick to be back in that jail, but they won't like it much. Now, get on out of here and let this man rest.'

22

The skinny clerk didn't notice Buck when he came in the front door to the hotel and, not wanting to interrupt what was obviously a delicate operation, the big cowboy didn't say anything. Slowly and taking great care, with the use of a mirror in one hand and a comb in the other, the man was smoothing what hair he had, trying to cover the baldest parts of his scalp. At last, unable to keep quiet any longer, Buck coughed.

'Oh, it ain't polite to sneak up on a man like that,' the clerk snarled, quickly hiding the brush and mirror on a shelf under the counter. 'I suppose you want the key to your room?'

'Yes, I suppose I do.'

'Well, I didn't know but what you'd left town. You ought to have said something. If I'd gotten busy and needed the room, I'd have gone ahead and rented it out.'

'And then you'd have had to move whoever you put there out,' Buck said, looking as stern as he could. 'I paid the rent through the rest of the week. Anyway, the day I have to tell you what I'm doing is the day one of us had better leave town. And I kind of like it here. Now, the key, if you please.'

'Well, you won't be so high and mighty when that good-for-nothing marshal gets a hold of you. The good people of this town have demanded that he do something about your helping that outlaw escape.'

'What outlaw?' Buck asked innocently. 'You don't mean Clarence Handy, do you?' When the clerk nodded, Buck just shook his head. 'What ever do you mean about Handy escaping? He just went for a little horseback ride. Doc Saunders has him back in his front bedroom and is taking care of him again.' As he turned toward the stairs he muttered just loud enough for the clerk to hear, 'I don't know where people get such crazy notions.'

He stopped by Vanessa's room, where he knocked and waited, but there was no answer. He'd go looking for her after getting a bath and clean clothes. The bed in his room was lumpy and housed the usual collection of bugs but for all that Buck thought it looked inviting. Sleeping outside was far better than in, but in his experience, few bedrolls ever were as comfortable as a bed. Maybe after a meal and a drink he'd end the day early.

Thinking about the drink led his mind straight to thinking about Molly Mae and his promise to take her on a picnic. Now that, he smiled, was something to consider.

Feeling better in a clean shirt, after a bath and barbershop shave at Harold Sims's place, he walked over to the restaurant. Sims had been a little friendlier than the hotel clerk but still had to get in his complaint about what Buck had done to help Handy escape.

'It's true, he may be an old-timer, and a sick old man at that,' Sims had argued as he lathered up Buck's face, 'but the fact remains he was found guilty and sentenced to hang. Now, I'm not saying it's right, but it is the law. You didn't do yourself any good in helping him get away, either.'

'Mr Sims,' Buck said, with the lower part of his face and neck covered with thick lather and before the barber started in with his long, finely honed straight razor, 'the old man was in danger from that man who called himself the state hangman. I only moved him to a place where he'd be safe. Now, before you let your anger get the better of you, let me say that Handy is back under Doc Saunders' care. You townspeople are sure hurting for excitement if the thought of missing out on a hanging upsets everybody so much.'

Holding Buck's head up with one finger and carefully scraping the two-days' beard off his chin, the barber went on with his commentary as if Buck hadn't said a word.

Stroking his smooth chin, Buck headed for the restaurant, smiling as he thought about people like Sims or that other one, Runkle.

'Well, so you did come back,' Marshal Coleman said by way of a greeting as he sat down in a chair across Buck's table. 'Vanessa said you'd be in tonight or tomorrow. She wouldn't say much more than that, but she was sure you'd show up.'

'I gather you've seen the young lady? I knocked on her hotel room door but she was out.'

'Yes, we just rode in a little bit ago. We spent most of the afternoon picnicking upriver.'

Buck smiled and waited until the waitress took his order before asking about the picnic.

'Never mind,' Coleman responded. 'I want to know exactly what you've been up to. I was putting away the horse I hired for Vanessa and saw your black in the stable corral so I knew you were back. And I've heard the story from both Vanessa and that little man, Newcomb. So unless you got something to add, we don't need to go through that again. But Vanessa said you went on out to the Plunkett ranch to find the man we thought was the hangman. What happened?'

'So you've decided old man Handy was right? That the first hangman really wasn't?'

'Yeah, after you and Vanessa left town I telegraphed the territorial capital. The description didn't fit the first man at all. Newcomb, the real Newcomb, said the man claiming to be the hangman was really called Cutter. I looked through my pile of Wanted posters and found one for someone called Gentleman Jack Cutter. No picture, just a description. It fit. There's a reward offered, so you got it coming, if you've got him stashed somewhere.'

Buck laughed. 'That's one reward that won't get collected, Marshal. Mr

Cutter has been stashed, all right, but he's in no shape to be brought in for identification.'

While Buck ate his meal of meatloaf and potatoes and gravy, Coleman sat taking his time over coffee and watched.

He let some time pass before giving up about what had happened with Cutter. 'That's all you're going to say about it?' he asked.

'Yeah, that's all. Cutter won't be coming around to bother Handy or anyone any more. Did anyone tell you that Handy is back at the doctor's house?'

'Yeah, Doc Saunders came out as we were riding in to tell us. Poor old Doc told Vanessa that he wasn't going to allow anyone to talk to the old man but he couldn't stop her. She left me to put the horses up and went running into the house. That's where she is now, I think.'

'Well, that's to be expected. That should make you and the local folks happy, having that big bad man back in custody. That's all I've heard since I rode in, how everybody feels cheated cause Handy escaped. Damn fools.'

Coleman nodded. 'I'm not sure you didn't break the law, taking him like that. But now that you brought him back, I guess it'll have to be forgotten. Oh, and there's one other thing that happened while you were gone. A telegram came for Vanessa.'

'Now who would be sending her a telegram? I don't suppose you happened to see what it was about, did you?'

'Well, you know how it is, there aren't that many telegrams come in for people here. And everybody knows the only way to keep a telegram private is not to send one, especially in a small town like this. But, yeah, it was bad news. Seems Vanessa's aunt passed away right after you two left Denver.'

'That is bad news.' Buck frowned, 'I suppose Vanessa will want to head back as soon as possible. Her aunt was about all the family she had, far as I know. Damn,' he said; then after a minute or so he looked up at the marshal. 'Well, on the bright side, at least she'll be gone when that skinny hangman takes Handy to the gallows.'

Coleman stared at the table a minute before nodding. 'Yeah, I guess.'

23

After paying for his meal, Buck invited the marshal over to the Past Time for a drink. Buck wasn't disappointed when the lawman decided he'd better spend some time in his office before calling it a day. Walking through the swinging doors, he stopped and let his eyes take in the long, smoke-filled room. Molly Mae wasn't in sight.

As he paid for his mug of frothy beer he saw that Amos was at his usual table, dealing poker to two other men. Buck decided he could afford to lose a few dollars and wandered over. Possibly he could find out when Molly Mae would be coming in.

Buck saw Amos watching him as he dealt a hand and simply nodded when Buck motioned toward the empty chair next to him. He sat down, put a few dollars on the table and leaned back to watch the play. The man across from him was the local businessman, Runkle, the other was someone Buck had never seen before.

'Well,' Runkle said, pulling in the pot after winning the hand, 'looks good to see you willing to leave a few dollars in town before you take off.'

Buck frowned. 'I didn't know I was taking off.'

'Well, it seems likely. Rumor has it that the young woman you're riding with, that relative of old man Handy, her aunt passed away back in Denver. I figure now that Handy is back, there won't be much reason for you to stick around.'

Amos finished shuffling the cards and then, tapping the deck on the table to get everyone's attention, waited until they had tossed in their ante. Buck smiled across the table. 'I don't know that one thing follows another. Not that it matters. I'm here to play a little poker, that's all.'

Runkle looked at the cards that had

been dealt to him and frowned. Looking up, he sneered. 'I don't think I want to play anymore. Somehow it just doesn't seem right that you're not in the jail you took Handy out of. There's a number of us who don't take to you getting away with helping the old fool escape.' He slammed his cards down on to the felt.

The third man tossed in his hand and shook his head. 'I'm like this fella,' he said directing his words at Runkle. 'All I want to do is play cards.'

Buck, being the last to throw in his cards, picked up the few coins in the pot. Amos picked up all the cards and held them ready to shuffle the deck. 'At this table that's what we do, play poker.' His voice sounded deep, like it came from somewhere down near the bottom of his big chest. Buck watched as his long supple fingers handled the cards, cutting and shuffling them in turn. Holding on to the deck, ready to deal another hand, he looked at each man in turn. 'Anyone wanting to argue or fight might as well go someplace else.'

Cursing, Runkle pushed away from the table, picked up his money and stomped out of the saloon.

'I didn't mean to chase away your players,' Buck said apologetically.

'You didn't. He's a poor poker-player and a worse loser. It doesn't help to have someone like that at the table. You two still playing?' Both nodded. 'Poker isn't a game for two players,' his words rumbled, 'so if you don't mind, I'll deal myself in.'

The men anted and for the next few hands the play went around the table with no one taking more to hand than they lost. Things changed when two men came in and made their way to the table. Buck hadn't noticed them because, at about the same time, Molly Mae came down the stairs.

Nodding to Amos, she spotted Buck and smiled before moving off toward the bar.

'She'll be moving around a while,' Amos said under his breath. 'It's something she does before settling at that high chair at the end of the bar. You've got time for a few more hands.' Buck glanced at the big man and saw he wasn't smiling as he dealt out the cards.

With four players, the dealer sat out, shuffling the cards and making sure the bets were right. Buck had been getting average cards, not anything great but good enough to stay in. Now the cards went against him. Hand after hand he anted, bet his cards before making his discard and then, not improving the pair or lone ace, tossed them in. Being aware of Molly Mae close by was the cause, he thought, until Amos brought the game to an abrupt halt.

Buck was fascinated by the flexibility of the dealer's long fingers as they sent the cards skimming across the felt. Each card landed in front of the player Amos was dealing to, always face down and ready to play. Picking up his cards and seeing he had nothing, Buck tossed them into the discard pile.

'Cards?' he asked the other men at the table.

Seeing Molly climb up on the high stool at the end of the bar, Buck picked up his coins, nodded at Amos and left the poker table.

'Man, that dealer of yours is fast,' he said to the longhaired woman. He took the hand she held out to him. Without being told, the bartender poured two glasses of pale-brown whiskey for them.

'Watch him closely,' she smiled, 'and you'll see that no matter how many men he's dealing to, he is watching everything that goes on in the room. I don't know how he does it, but it pays off. There hasn't been one fight in here since he took over that table. Now, tell me about what you've been doing. The story is you brought Handy back to Doc Saunders's house.'

Buck smiled. Sipping the smooth liquor he told her about the ride out to the Plunkett ranch, leaving out any mention of being trapped in the mine shaft and the shooting of Cutter. 'Yes, the old man is back in bed and, I hope, feeling better. From what I could tell, the couple days he spent outside didn't hurt him at all.'

'Doc Saunders didn't understand why I kept pouring the brandy, and now he's not saying one thing about it. I'm glad you're back. Now, invite me on that picnic you promised to take me on.'

'Marshal Coleman apparently took Vanessa on a picnic earlier today. Somewhere a little way up along the river, or so he said.'

'I think I know the place. It's where young couples go to get away from people. As I recall, I had offered to pack the food and you were going to get a buggy. You can drive a buggy, can't you?'

Buck laughed. 'I can drive a buggy. And getting away from people is what I'd call a good idea.' He sipped the whiskey, almost choking on it when she put a hand on his arm and chuckled.

'OK, then.' She laughed at his

discomfort. 'Let's go early, say about eleven? I rarely get to bed before midnight and every woman needs to get enough sleep.' Thinking he'd agree to anything she wanted, Buck merely nodded. 'I'll be ready. But now, it's back to making my customers happy. Are you going to go back to the poker game?'

'No, I think it's time for me to bed down. Lately it seems every day has been overly full. This whiskey is just about all I can handle. I will be out front in the morning.'

Outside in the night air, he stopped to roll a cigarette, breathing the cool night air in deeply before striking a match. He climbed up on to the hotel porch and sat down in one of the rockers to finish his smoke. When the hotel door opened he looked round and came to his feet as Vanessa came out into the evening.

'There you are,' she said, pulling another chair over. 'I waited for you and when you didn't come up to your room I thought I'd probably find you over at the saloon.'

'A proper young lady wouldn't go into a saloon, especially at night.'

'Well, maybe, but one would if she wanted to talk with you. But now I don't need to, do I?' She smiled in the weak light that came streaming through the hotel window. 'That seems to be your favorite chair and I'm not surprised to find you here.'

'Well, you know what they say, never walk when you can ride, and never stand when you can sit. Marshal Coleman told me about your Aunt Elizabeth, I'm purely sorry.'

'Thank you. The telegram was a shock, all right. She was like a mother to me and was always so strong, even lately when she wasn't feeling good. But, well, at least now I won't have to tell her about Uncle Clarence.' They were quiet for a while. Buck finished his smoke and, after pinching out the lit end, he flipped the butt out into the street. Not knowing what he could say, he leaned back and waited for her.

'That's one of the things I wanted to talk to you about, Buck. Uncle Clarence. He didn't tell me anything about that man, Cutter, other than to say he wouldn't be bothering anyone any more.'

Buck didn't say anything, just nodded his head. 'Well,' she went on after waiting a minute, 'I guess that's good news. If you came back and he didn't, it's good.'

'I found the cache that your uncle told you about. It's up in my room in the bottom of my saddle-bags. I didn't have a chance to tell Handy much about it. He was a little scared that you wouldn't want to have anything to do with it, I mean, it being stolen and all.'

Vanessa was silent. 'Was it where Uncle Clarence said it'd be?'

'Yeah, it was just where you were told it'd be, in some kind of natural hole in the fork of an old tree. From the looks of the tin box it was in, I'd say it'd been there a while. Mostly it was in two canvas bags, one full of ten-dollar gold coins and the other one filled with jewelry. Your uncle asked me to figure out what to do with it all, and here's what I think. The coins, well, I don't know as I'd trust too many people with the coins. Some of the watches and things might be identified, but even then, I figure it'll be hard to return the jewelry back to its owners.'

'Should we try to do that, find the owners?'

'The way I see it, there is no way anyone could lay claim to the coins. There weren't any markings on the canvas bags and one coin looks a lot like the next. The Plummer gang was said to have been in a lot of hold-ups, so figuring out who owns the coins would not be likely. The jewelry is something else. Say someone saw a necklace and recognized it as belonging to Grandma. Well, that could happen.'

'What do you have in mind, then?'

'How about you keep the sack of gold coins and I turn the jewelry over to the marshal. He wouldn't have to know anything about where it all came from or even whether that was all of it. I don't imagine anyone knows whether you're likely to be carrying around a lot of money or not, so if you don't tell anyone, then that gold could go a long way.'

'Aren't you going to take any of it?'

'Naw, what would I want with gold? I've got enough in my pocket to take care of me, and there's still the money for our return fare. I figure those coins should be yours. Without your aunt, you'll have to make your own way, so they'll come in handy.'

Vanessa sat for a while, rocking back gently back and forth. 'There's something else, Buck,' she said after a while. 'William Tell asked me to marry him. Now,' she stopped rocking and leaned forward, her words coming fast, 'I realize we haven't known each other long, but . . . ' she stopped. 'And I think, well, I think I'll say yes.'

Buck didn't say anything, just rocked

back and forth for a bit. 'My ma said she and pa got married after only seeing each other in church a few times,' Buck said softly. 'They were married, well, I don't know how long. I've got a whole bunch of brothers and a sister or two, all back in Texas. I guess it doesn't matter how long people know each other,' he finished, thinking about Molly Mae.

'I told him I'd have to talk to you, but I've already decided to say yes. I'll have to go back to Denver to close down Aunt Elizabeth's house, but that could be our honeymoon trip, couldn't it?'

'Vanessa, I think you could do a lot worse than the marshal. He strikes me as a good man.' Blocking a yawn with his hand, he got up. 'Now, with all that out of the way, I think it's time for me to go in. I've got a big day tomorrow.'

It was Vanessa's turn to laugh. 'I know. William Tell told me that you had promised to take Miss Molly on a picnic. He said you're taking her where we went this morning.' She laughed. 'You be careful, Buck. That's a beautiful picnic place and it's where William Tell proposed to me. You watch what you say to her.'

24

The picnic was everything Buck could want. In the morning he had spent time at the livery, running a curry comb over the coat of a good-looking chestnut mare until its light-brown skin gleamed in the morning sun. Brushing out the animal's long tail and mane only took a little longer and was worth it, he figured. He had decided to use the stable horse to pull the rented buggy, giving his black horse a little rest. Both the black and Cutter's mustang were in the back corral, ignoring each other.

Buck could hardly take his eyes off Molly Mae when he stopped to pick her up. She joked that it was the large wicker basket filled with food and drink that he was really interested in. He placed the basket and a tightly covered wooden barrel in the back of the buggy before handing her on to the seat. Her long flowing skirt hid a pair of dainty black leatherette boots, the toes peeking out as she made herself comfortable on the black leather seat. Her white cotton shirtwaist had double rows of pearl buttons running up the front, ending in a neat narrow-banded collar. It was dazzling white even in the shade of the buggy's top.

Even the mare seemed to know this was a special ride, stepping high and almost dainty as they rode at a steady trot out of town and along the river. Following Molly's directions, Buck reined off the well-used road and on to a twin-rutted wagon trail that ended in a small meadow. The river, moving wide and slow, curved in a large sweep around the grassy spot. Not a cloud marred the deep blue of the sky and although it had seemed hot back in town, the flowing water kept the noontime air comfortable.

While Molly spread out a large colorful blanket and started emptying the basket, Buck unhitched the horse and, after slipping on hobbles, turned it out to graze.

'It isn't often I get a chance to cook,' Molly remarked, placing golden brown-coated pieces of fried chicken on a plate. A big bowl of potato salad, thick-cut slices of homemade bread and a fresh-smelling pie was laid out for Buck's inspection.

'You had better not let anyone back in town know about this or they'll all be wanting to eat at your place and not the restaurant.'

The wooden barrel, he discovered, was filled with glass-stoppered bottles of beer, kept cool by chunks of ice. 'Now this is unexpected.' Buck smiled as he poured two glasses of the brew. 'Going on picnics with you is a real treat.' Lifting his glass, he toasted the woman before taking a sip that left a white beer-mustache on his upper lip.

After eating their fill of the food, drinking another glass or so of the beer, they walked down to the river's edge. Molly found a large boulder to sit on while Buck picked up a handful of small rocks and started tossing them into the water.

'I guess I should have brought a pole and some worms,' he said, pointing across to the far bank where the water looked to be moving faster. 'It's a sure thing there's a couple big old lunkers hiding over there.'

He finished tossing the stones and turned to her. 'How did you ever come to end up here in French Gulch? Not that it's any of my business, you understand.'

Molly laughed. 'It's no big secret,' she said. 'I was living with my father in a small town back East when one day a man all duded up in a black suit came into our store. He introduced himself as Fred Ralston. A small businessman, he said. Father knew at once he was a gambler, but I didn't. All I saw was his soft hands and clear, smiling eyes. Every other man in town had work-roughened hands and looked at me as if I were a slab of meat in the market.'

She stopped a minute before going on.

'Father tried to warn me, but Fred said all the things a girl wants to hear. When he left town — I heard later it was just before he was going to be run out — he asked me to go with him. I did. We were married in the next town and for the next few years we had a good life. He gambled and I . . . well mostly I sat and waited. But it was a good time. His gambling meant we could spend our days together. Whenever we'd move on to another town I never paid any attention to the why of it. Come a morning he'd say it was time and we'd just pack up and move.'

Laughing, she shook her head. 'Oh, I guess I knew he was a crooked gambler and that someday he'd get caught. But he loved me and treated me like a queen. He had hit a good streak and we came here and bought out the owner of the Past Time. We should have kept going, I suppose. Fred tried one of his tricks to the wrong man and was shot. The man who shot him came and apologized later. It was sweet of him and I think he was surprised that I was so calm about it. Anyway, now I run the saloon with Amos's help and it's a profitable business. Now, tell me about you.'

Buck was silent for a bit, then nodded. 'Just your typical cowboy, I guess. I own my horse, my saddle and my six-gun and not much else. I'm the youngest of a pretty big family. When my pa died, the older brothers took over and, well, I rode off. Some day I might go back to ranching, but for now, I just like to see what's over there.' He threw a thumb over his shoulder.

'A cowboy who is about to lose his bodyguard job, from what I hear.'

'Yeah. Vanessa's a good young woman and I think they'll make a good marriage.' Thinking about what the end of his reason of staying in the area meant, he ducked his head and didn't say anything else.

'Well,' Molly said, 'it's getting along and I still have to clean this up before opening the saloon tonight. We had better be getting back.'

Buck hadn't noticed, but checking where the sun was he saw that most of the afternoon had slipped away.

The ride back to town was quicker than the ride out and they were in front of the Past Time before he was ready for it. As Buck was giving Molly Mae a hand down, Amos came out the front door. Buck started to unload the picnic basket and the beer barrel. Without a word, the big man picked the picnic things up and went back inside.

'Thank you, Molly Mae,' Buck said, touching the brim of his hat. 'I'll return this wagon to the stable and stop by for a drink later.'

Smiling at him, she nodded and disappeared through the swinging doors.

Buck rode on down to the stable and helped the old man unhitch the buggy, leaving it out back. As he walked up the street toward the hotel room, he spotted a group of men going into the barbershop. Must be having a sale on haircuts, he mused.

Going past the restaurant, he saw Vanessa and Marshal Coleman seated at a table and decided a cup of coffee might be in order.

'Hey, there,' he called going through the door. 'Is that private family stuff you're talking about, or can an out-of-work bodyguard sit in?'

Laughing, Coleman pushed a chair out. 'We were just discussing things we've got to do,' he said. 'I didn't know getting married was so complicated.'

'Well, I'll tell you the truth, Marshal. I figure there will be a lot of things you'll be discovering you didn't know about.'

'Buck,' Vanessa objected, 'don't be telling him that or he'll change his mind.'

'Oh, I doubt that. But listen, there is one thing we should talk about. That mustang I brought back to town, I don't imagine anyone will be coming up and laying claim to that horse. I don't have a bill of sale and the previous owner isn't about to come up and complain. Seems like a good animal. If it were up to me, I'd say the little mare would make a good riding-horse for the future Mrs Coleman.'

Marshal Coleman nodded, but before he could say anything the front door slammed open and Doc Saunders came rushing in. 'Marshal, you'd better come quick. Clarence is having a tough time of it.'

With a pale-faced Vanessa following right behind, the lawman left the restaurant. Buck finished the coffee he'd ordered and, after deciding he didn't need supper, he got up and headed for his hotel room. If the old man was worse it was the marshal's place, he thought, to sympathize with Vanessa. He no longer had that job.

Using the water in the pitcher in his room, Buck washed up a little before lying back on the bed, where he fell asleep. A little later he came awake and glanced out the window to see how dark it had gotten. He'd slept longer than he expected to. Well, he thought smiling, it'll be about time to go have a drink with Molly.

He changed into his freshly washed shirt, strolled across to the saloon and pushed through to find the place nearly empty. There was no sign of Molly. Amos, sitting at his usual table, nodded and the bartender moved down to where he stopped at the bar.

'Beer, I guess,' Buck ordered, before turning to lean his back against the wood. He was about half-finished with his drink when Molly came hurrying through the front doors, not smiling.

'Buck, you've got to get out of here,' she said, stress hurrying her words.

'Whoa, there, lady,' he said, holding out a hand to touch her arm. 'Why do I have to leave? I just got here.'

Turning to call to Amos, she didn't answer Buck. 'Amos, go out the back door and down to the stable. Put a saddle on Buck's black horse and bring it to the back. Don't let anyone see you.' Not waiting to argue, the big man disappeared out the back. At another word from her the bartender went to stand in the front doors.

'That black stud horse more'n likely won't let Amos near him,' Buck said, shaking his head. 'But what's this all about?'

'Clarence Handy died a little bit ago,' she said. 'I was over at the marshal's office, to see if there was anything I could do for Vanessa. She's taking it well; I guess she must've expected it.'

'Yeah, I reckon. It'll be for the best, though; she won't have to face him getting hung.'

'That's the problem. Runkle and the barber, Sims, and some of the others were working themselves up to go carry out the hanging. They were meeting and had formed some kind of vigilante committee when they heard the old man had died. They stormed over to the marshal's office to make sure it was true. When Runkle saw Vanessa, he turned on her saying both she and you should be held for having helped

Handy escape. Marshal Coleman is talking to them now. He says that decision is not for them to decide. It's something for the district judge to deal with.'

'Well, that sounds likely.'

'Not to Runkle. He wants someone to hang. That's why you have to get out of here now. They are talking about coming for you.'

Amos came though the back door and nodded at Buck. 'Your horse is all ready,' he said before sitting back down at his poker table.

Buck could only shake his head. 'Well, I never heard the like.'

'Buck,' Molly said, fear starting to show in her voice, 'you've got to go while you can. There's too many of them and if you stay someone will get hurt and I don't want it to be you. Is there anything in your hotel room you can't do without?'

'No, I just put on my cleanest shirt. There's nothing up there but some dirty clothes and a few personal things.

But I'm not sure I'm ready to leave here now. Our picnic today was too much fun.'

Taking both his hands in hers, she looked him directly in the eye. 'Buck, it was a great day, and I enjoyed it a lot. But you're not the kind of man to settle down. Not now and not here. Like I said, I don't want anyone hurt, especially you.'

Buck slowly nodded. She was right. He no longer had any reason to hang around. It would only cause trouble for her and the marshal. Vanessa would be taken care of and no longer needed him. Maybe it was time to ride on.

Putting an arm around Molly, he hugged her close, kissing her hard. As he let her go, the bartender came running back saying the vigilantes were coming down the street.

'I think they locked the marshal in one of his cells and they're coming for you. They got blood in their eyes. You'd better not be here when they come through those doors.'

'Buck,' Molly said, looking up at him, fear in her eyes, 'I can maybe slow them down a little, but I won't be able to stop them. I don't want to see anyone killed, you or them, and that's what'll happen.'

'OK, Miss Molly,' Buck said. 'I'm gone. You take care of yourself and don't be surprised if one day I don't come walking through your doors again.' As he turned away, he called out to Amos, 'You take good care of her, old son.'

Without a backward glance, he pushed through the back door and stepped into the saddle.

'Darn it, horse, I'm not so sure I'm ready to ride,' he complained as he reined away and touched a heel to the black horse's side. As usual, he didn't get any answer from the animal.

THE END